# GOODBYE
# PARIS,
# SHALOM
# TEL
# AVIV

# GOODBYE PARIS, SHALOM TEL AVIV

## MARCO KOSKAS

TRANSLATED from the FRENCH by DAVID BALL

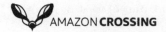

Text copyright © 2018 by Marco Koskas
Translation copyright © 2020 by David Ball
All rights reserved.

Previously published as *Bande de français* by the author in France in 2018. Translated from French by David Ball. First published in English by Amazon Crossing in 2020.

Published by Amazon Crossing, Seattle

www.apub.com

Amazon, the Amazon logo, and Amazon Crossing are trademarks of Amazon.com, Inc., or its affiliates.

ISBN-13: 9781542008464
ISBN-10: 1542008468

Cover design by Patrick Barry / Laserghost

Printed in the United States of America

*To Jo Amar*

# CHAPTER 1

The new Jerusalem streetcar line is modern, fast, and frequent. One every four minutes and at rush hour, every two minutes on average. It took years of work and caused huge traffic jams that exasperated the shopkeepers and neighbors of Yafo Street, but today all those annoyances are no more than a bad memory. It's been up and running since September 2011. Finally. And it's changed the landscape. People have even forgotten how Jerusalem was before the tram. Or without a tram.

Only, nobody's very relaxed on the cars. It's too bad—all that hatred between Jews and Arabs, that distrust and paranoia. Yet terrorist attacks are extremely rare on the line. Two or three cars rammed at the Beit Hanina and Shuafat stops on the northern section, but never stabbings inside like every day in town and in the Occupied Territories for the last few years. No one knows why, exactly. Maybe down deep, the Jews and Arabs of Jerusalem think of the streetcar as their common possession and it's better to preserve it. Intifadas come and go, the streetcar remains . . .

Juliette takes it Saturday night after Shabbat as she comes back from Pisgat Ze'ev, and she fearlessly takes a window seat because even if an Arab throws a rock as the trolley goes by, it won't break the window. They say it was designed for that. The tram's windowpanes were megareinforced.

It will take her twenty-five minutes to get to the bus station, where she's going to get the 490 bus to Tel Aviv. For tonight, Juliette is saying her final farewells to Jerusalem. Her farewells to the museum came at the end of the day before yesterday. Five years of managing the reserves under the supervision of Aviva Morgenstern, you really had to hold up! Above all, not break down . . . still, at her going-away party, she did pay tribute to her boss's great professionalism, her human qualities, her culture, and that old nut Aviva couldn't hold back her tears.

Juliette will return to Jerusalem, of course. It's the city she has in her heart, the city of her childhood and her first loves—her mother's city, her sister Mathilde's, her brother Assaf's, and her girlfriends' city too. Sure, she'll come back, but no more than every third Shabbat because even if Shabbat at Mathilde's in Pisgat Ze'ev is nice, it's very restrictive. No smoking, no phoning, what a pain! Luckily, Juliette adores her nephews. Seven kids in twelve years, you have to admire her. She had the first at twenty-two and the last one six months ago, at the age of thirty-four; the next one will be when God wills. With the Orthodox, women have six kids on average. So there's nothing unusual about it, except that Juliette's already twenty-nine and she's nowhere near having a kid. Not the ghost of the chance of a first one on the horizon. What a difference between the two of them! It's funny, two sisters so unlike each other. To be precise: two half sisters.

Juliette did promise herself to have at least one child before she turned thirty, but since she's been with Elias, the odds are she won't keep that promise. The fact that he suggested she live with him in Tel Aviv is already unbelievable. Unhoped for. Practically a godsend! Makes her believe he loves her like when you really love someone. She met him in Jerusalem the year before, and at the beginning he didn't even want people to see them together. She was living in a studio apartment in Nahalat Shiva and he was in Gilo, in a new development. When he slept at her place, he ran off before the sun came up. A wild one, Elias. But there you are, Juliette loves his wildness. When he first came to Jerusalem, he slept in parks, out in the open, so in love with Israel that he'd live there like a beggar without complaining, and hungry most of the time to boot.

When he left Jerusalem, Juliette thought he was only going to live in Tel Aviv to get away from her. But no. Finally, he cares more about her than she thought. Despite his degree in petrochemical engineering and his acceptance by FEMIS, the prestigious French film school, Elias wants to be a journalist while waiting to write his first novel. He changes vocations regularly. At thirty-four, he's still trying to find himself and that worries his family. But what about Henry Miller? At what age did he become a novelist? Elias worships Henry Miller, that's obvious. He's reread *The Rosy Crucifixion* three times, and he always has one of the three parts of the trilogy on him: *Sexus*, *Plexus*, or *Nexus* is forever peeping out of his pocket. On the other hand, he reads and rereads Céline on the sly, because hey, reading that anti-Semitic sonofabitch in the country of the Jews is really pushing it. His pal Manu gave him the *Voyage* illustrated by Tardi, and Elias leafs through it practically every night, both enchanted and mortified by Céline's genius. Some Jews' taste for Céline is hard to explain, but at least Manu has a theory about his anti-Semitism. He always quotes the passage in *Death on the Installment Plan* where Céline talks about his father, a clerk in an insurance company, who was fired after the invention of typewriters. And Céline imitates him, accusing the Jews of having invented those diabolical machines.

That's where Manu's theory comes from: Céline's anti-Semitism is simply an inability to be different from the father. Whew! Elias loves that theory. He loves Manu. Between those two, the three topics of conversation are, in order of importance, Céline, women, and Céline.

Manu, too, made his aliyah three years ago, who knows why. He was doing great as an actor in hard-core adult movies in Paris, but he got sick of it. Understandable, after thirty years of porn. A four-month stay in Jerusalem, but the city's a little too spiritual for a guy with a CV like his, a bit too drenched in the sacred. Even when he's parking a car, Manu carries around with him his old, dirty past and definitely prefers Tel Aviv. At least there he can talk about his career without shocking anybody.

Anyway, Juliette's making the big leap this evening. She doesn't know Tel Aviv very well aside from Metzitzim Beach and a few hip bars in Neve Tzedek. She doesn't know many people there, either, aside from Elias and his buddies. They're all thirtysomethings except for Manu and Diabolo. And hopelessly French. Likeable, but megamacho. Actually, Juliette's French too. But she's always lived in Jerusalem, that's the difference, aside from her four years at the École du Louvre in Paris. Wonderful memories. All those museums, that vibrant Parisian life. Living among those nymphs and sylphs suited her. She resembles them so much! As angelic as a Botticelli but with the freshness of Sandrine Bonnaire in *À Nos Amours*. And that very ephemeral grace girls between sixteen and eighteen sometimes have.

A real pietà, that Juliette, but with curves like Bar Refaeli.

She calls Elias to tell him she'll be at his place in less than two hours, and she secretly hopes he'll offer to pick her up with his scooter at Tachana Merkazit because Tel Aviv's central bus station is in a rough part of town: Sudanistan, as the papers say. But Elias seems to have his head somewhere else.

5

He repeats, "OK, doll. OK, great, I'll wait for you," with his exasperating way of openly thinking of something else when she talks to him, without even trying to hide it. Finally, Juliette hangs up, disappointed, even slightly bitter, and she doesn't notice the feverish Arab slipping in between the standing passengers. Just at the moment he's about to throw himself at her and stick a knife in her chest, there's the sound of an explosion and the guy's carotid explodes in a thousand pieces of red flesh that spatter on the ceiling of the car at the same time his eyes pop out of their sockets. He drops his knife and collapses on Juliette, drenching her with his blood. It all happens at once. Life, death, screams—ordinary life in Jerusalem.

The blond soldier who fired rushes over the fallen Arab to free Juliette. The streetcar stops, and already the sirens can be heard far away. Shaking and covered with blood, Juliette staggers to the door.

"You *beseder*?" the soldier calls out to her in Frebrew while she keeps an eye on the body on the ground.

"The doors!" someone yells in real Hebrew, and suddenly the doors open.

Juliette leaves the car gasping for air, while the first-aid workers pop out of the night in their fluorescent jackets. They push her into the ambulance, although she's safe and sound. *Beseder*, she's OK, but still . . . off to the ER of Hadassah Medical Center. During the ride, they clean up her face and arms and ask her a few questions to see if she's disoriented. Suddenly she pops up on the stretcher.

"My suitcase!"

"Don't worry, *motek*, they'll bring it back to you, honey," a blue-eyed paramedic reassures her.

"But I need it right away! I'm leaving Jeru! I'm going to live in Tel Aviv! With Elias!"

"Don't worry, *motek*," the guy repeats. "You got to see the docs first."

"But you *know* they're gonna blow it up, that's what they do with abandoned luggage!"

"We'll bring it back to you at the hospital, I promise you." The guy calls his coworkers who're still there and tells them to put Juliette's case aside. Juliette falls heavily back on the stretcher, grumbling. This day of all days, just her luck! Victim of a knife attack the day she's going to start a new life and—who knows—have a kid with Elias. She rummages in her clothes unsuccessfully and sits up on the stretcher again.

"My phone!"

"There," the blue-eyed guy says, showing her the old, beat-up Sony she's holding in her hand. But she can't see it. Typical posttraumatic stress. You lose your bearings. She finally manages to call Elias, but she gets his voice mail. "Darling, I almost died in a terrorist attack, I almost almost almost died," she repeats with tears in her eyes. "I almost got stabbed, Elias! For you! To go live with you! I love you so much, why don't you answer me?" She starts sobbing, letting herself go in voice mail. Everything goes into it: she is a bastard, unloved, the whole nine yards.

They put her under observation.

Her mother arrives in Hadassah, panic stricken. How long has she wanted to leave this country? What the hell is she still doing here, for godsake? If she stays, it's only for Juliette. But at the idea of losing her daughter in a stabbing attack, she feels herself capable of the worst. At the same time, it's just an expression going through her mind—"capable of the worst." What worst? In the fiery mouth of Juliette's father, that had some style, not in hers. She's using the expression without really knowing its meaning, out of blind faithfulness to her great love, like a quotation or, better still, an incantation— almost a prayer to God the Father.

An hour later, Juliette begins rummaging in her things again.

"Where the hell did I put my phone?"

"In your hand, dear," her mother answers.

She calls Elias again, and again gets his voice mail. This time she hangs up and sends him a text full of affliction and tears: *Don't abandon me, Elias, please. U can't know how scared I was. I had a date w death, can u imagine? Before I even had a kid w u! I beg u, call back! Call quick! Wanna hear yr voice. I want yr child!*

# CHAPTER 2

Elias reads this as he gets to Florentin 10 and sighs. Why did he say she could come? All he wants to do is write a novel, not get married or even be a couple. That's clear enough, isn't it?

He sits down at the table with Manu and the anorexic whose name he can never remember. Oh yeah, Scarlett! She's funny, has style, always in a dress and high heels, but all skin and bones. They'd think she was kind of snobbish if she weren't a fan of the Hapoel Tel Aviv, the lefty working-class soccer club. But Scarlett goes to every Hapoel game at Bloomfield Stadium. It's like a bourgeois girl from Neuilly who's wild about the Red Star, slumming it to catch every match.

"Bad news?" she asks in Hebrew, since Elias learned the language well.

"A knife attack in Jeru," he answers. "The victim's a friend." And to Manu in a low voice, "It's Juliette."

"Huh? Juliette? She's dead?" Manu asks.

"No, no," Elias answers flatly, and you'd think at that moment he'd rather have answered yes. Well, not a real death that ends life, but let's say a symbolic death that would make Juliette disappear from his life. When there's no way of breaking off with a girl, you think of her death, why not? But then, what's the point of having her come and giving her hope again if he's thinking of ending it? Why keep her in that cruel illusion?

"Where's she now?" asks Manu.

"In Hadassah."

"So when's she coming?"

"Um, I don't know."

"She hurt?"

"I'm telling you she's OK."

"Serious?"

"What are you, deaf?" Elias says angrily. "OK means OK! But she's under observation in the hospital."

They order a bottle of Merlot. At thirty-six shekels a glass, you might as well get a bottle since that makes six glasses in all, so two each, you're saving around thirty-six shekels. Nine euros, in fact. Since the euro began sinking, it's still more expensive. In Tel Aviv, you really shell out for red! And not only French red. The Israelis have begun making wine too. And good wine! In fact, it seems the word *Chardonnay* is the French pronunciation of a Jerusalem vine that was called *Char Adonai*, in other words "the mountain of God." But that must be a Zionist joke.

Just then, Diabolo calls Manu about a job as a reporter on *Israel Breaking News*, and Manu tells him for the $n$th time the only thing he knows how to do is be a professional fucker, and besides, he dropped out of the profession. So naturally he asks Diabolo if he keeps offering him the job just to bug him.

"Come on, I'm kidding around, it's just because I'm having a barbecue tonight and Romy Schneider will be there."

"You swear?"

"Word of honor."

"OK, I'm coming with Elias and a girl you don't know."

"Juliette?"

"No, no, Juliette's in the hospital. She almost died in a stabbing attack."

"What! An attack in Jeru?"

"Yes, in Jeru."

"But that's a scoop! Send Elias to interview her!" Manu turns to Elias, who waves no to him with his forefinger.

"You kidding?" Diabolo says, offended. "What've you got against the press?"

"All sleazebags," Manu answers, laughing.

"Put Elias on the line!"

There follows a laborious back-and-forth between Diabolo, who wants his exclusive interview with Juliette-the-miraculous-survivor, and Elias, who refuses to give in. It's true that since he has the victim's number and a personal relationship with her, Elias could make an incredible scoop for the new agency.

It would also give him a good start as a reporter. Only, there you are, he obstinately refuses to have this piece of luck serve Diabolo's ends. No way his relationship with Juliette's going to become official by writing about her. To hell with the pathos! He really digs his heels in. This said, he also has no faith in *Israel Breaking News*. He's even sure it's going to totally crash. There are already so many francophone blogs in Israel. Do we really need another media outlet for such a small market?

All the same, Elias could make an effort, just out of friendship for Diabolo. No. He does not want to work for Diabolo or interview Juliette.

"OK, so would you give me her number, so I can do the interview myself?"

"Stop it, she knows we're buddies."

"I'll get someone she doesn't know to call her, OK?"

"Who?"

"Jonathan. They don't know each other, right?"

"Which Jonathan?"

"Simsen."

"OK, all right." And Elias finally gives him the number.

"Great, thanks, Eli. See you soon at the barbecue?"

Elias sighs. "It's nine already."

"Life begins at midnight." Diabolo laughs and hangs up.

Man, she's sticking to him like a leech. Like a piece of gum on your shoe. She's invading his life, she's even annexing his friends with her bad luck. Elias doesn't realize his own good luck. A beauty like Juliette, most guys would crawl on their knees to get her. Hey, Jonathan Simsen!

After the phone interview, he gets a selfie from Juliette in her hospital bed, and it floors him.

"You see that bombshell?" Jonathan says to Diabolo, whose face darkens.

"Don't give me that crap, Jojo, she's Elias's woman!" Diabolo answers, with that godfather frown that sometimes crosses his face, and Jonathan shuts up fast. But Diabolo's best argument is his build, of course. Weighing in at over three hundred pounds inspires a certain respect. But still, he'd better lose at least a third of it. If he's not going to put a ring in his stomach, he absolutely has to slim down. All that bad fat could screw up his coronary arteries. Forty-eight's the ideal age for a heart attack.

# CHAPTER 3

They can smell grilling meat before reaching Diabolo's place. It's spreading through all the Yemenite neighborhood of Kerem HaTeimanim that evening. Elias's mouth waters and Scarlett gets nauseous, while Manu is almost feverish at the idea of meeting Romy Schneider. But he doesn't show it at all. She's finally back after two months of immersion in the kibbutz at Beit El to improve her Hebrew. And also to save money, since she rented her apartment on Dizengoff Avenue to tourists through Airbnb. On the other hand, the torture is going to begin for Manu. There are women who get wildly excited when they learn he was a porn actor, as if that guarantees he's a great lay. Not Romy, though. She doesn't give a damn about his sexual talents. Anyway, she's not looking to date right now. She's told him twenty times. Poor Manu, he's still crazy about her. And then he knows very well that no woman goes for long without screwing. She must have some guy here in Tel Aviv. But who? Who is the lucky sonofabitch?

On the terrace, Diabolo's box of Havanas has pride of place in the middle of the table. Elias digs out two Cohibas right away and puts one in his mouth, the other in his shirt pocket, without hiding or standing on ceremony. He helps himself to meat without excessive politeness, either, a heaping plate, because he hasn't eaten anything since yesterday noon. He skips meals often, but he never talks about it or else he makes a joke out if it: "I skip meals more than I skip screwing girls." Poor Elias, a Don Juan with a postgraduate degree—but undernourished. Diabolo on the job, Elias stuffing himself, Manu like a little virgin with Romy, Scarlett and Jonathan Simsen yakking away in Hebrew in a corner, that's the atmosphere of the terrace as the evening starts up. In the sky dotted with stars, the full moon gives the Royal Beach Hotel a halo of silvery particles, and it seems that new residence for billionaires is throwing out more sparkles than usual through the stellar haze. Since Royal Beach was erected along the Tayelet promenade, the only bit of sea that used to be visible from Diabolo's place has been blocked. The Tel Aviv landscape changes every day. No ocean view can be guaranteed. They're building everywhere.

"Bring us up two more bottles of red, Jonathan!" Diabolo calls out to the company at large, and the young apprentice reporter immediately rushes down the stairs to get the wine in the kitchen.

"Stop treating him like that," whispers Romy, irritated.

"What the hell!" Diabolo says, mocking her. "At least *he* doesn't mind working with me." A hardly veiled allusion to Elias's refusal to work at *Israel Breaking News*.

Elias answers right back from his seat on the wicker sofa: "Hey, don't complain, thanks to me, *IBN* got its first scoop!"

"Roger that," Diabolo says graciously. "I guarantee you, with Juliette's picture bringing people in, they'll pick up that piece everywhere."

Someone named Sandy arrives on the terrace at that moment. She's an apprentice reporter at *Israel Breaking News*, too, and she walks right up to Elias. As if she's teleguided. Or magnetized. Really, he attracts them like flies. A half hour of conversation and she's literally sprawled all over him. He lets himself go without thinking of Juliette anymore. Well, yes, he does think of her a little bit. But reluctantly. Besides, it looks like couples are forming fast this evening: you can see Diabolo and Scarlett getting much closer even if their respective sizes pose a small problem. Laurel and Hardy are fine for movie farces, not for ill-matched couples. As for Manu, he finally dares to look Romy in the eyes. With the help of the wine, he even begins to kid around and make her laugh. At one moment, he takes her hand, and she gives him a tender yet irritated look. "How many times do I have to tell you I don't feel like it?" she whispers to him, smiling. Smiling, for once.

17

Usually, she's brusque with him. Nonetheless, Romy agrees to let him walk her back to Dizengoff Avenue.

From Kerem to her place takes a good thirty minutes on the Tayelet promenade along the seaside. In general, that creates a connection, and sometimes, even when the girl isn't exactly filled with desire, she finally accepts, just so as not to sleep alone or even out of weariness. Manu's kind of counting on that. It's really a shame she doesn't want him, because they'd make a fine couple. Despite his sixty years, Manu has a natural casualness that's extremely intriguing, a real detachment, and Romy—well, Romy makes you think irresistibly of Romy Schneider. And she's already over fifty, so they're almost the same age. You'd think they're a couple out of a Claude Sautet movie. Once they're in front of her door, he tells her timidly that he's writing a screenplay with her as the heroine.

"You're crazy, Manu!" she exclaims. "You're a nutball! What do you know about me to write a screenplay about me?"

"I know the main thing."

"Stop it . . . and since when are you a screenwriter? You just did X-rated movies, that's not film."

"You have to hurt me?"

"Sorry. It's touching, that you're writing about me, I guess, but you see . . . but . . . how can I say this? You see, I just want us to be friends."

"Well, that's just it, it's the story of a chick who just wants to be a pal of the guy who's crazy about her. A real classic, right?"

As for Elias, he has no problem bringing Sandy back to his little pad at the corner of Levinsky and Herzl in Florentin. Hardly have they arrived downstairs than they're already upstairs and Elias is digging around between her thighs. At least this Sandy isn't modest like Juliette. Juliette always burst out laughing when he licked her, as if he were tickling her. Sandy likes it so much she's moaning, and Elias doesn't stop until six in the morning, dead drunk from coming. A girl who likes having a guy go down on her, that's so rare! Well, no, there are lots of others. But man, what a change from the ticklish Juliette.

Instead of going calmly back to Florentin, Manu grabs Romy on her doorstep and kisses her on the mouth despite her resistance. He sticks in his tongue, she pushes him away, but he wraps her in his arms. She struggles, but he throws her back on the couch at the entrance and rips off her panties. He's going off his rocker. His demon's got hold of him again without warning, and he forces her thighs apart. Just when he's going to penetrate her, she sticks her thumb in his eye. Then he lets go.

"Get the hell out of here!" she yells, wild with rage, when he's already outside, holding his hand over his eye that's dripping with blood. "Get out of here, you loser! Don't let me see you again!"

"Want to do it sitting down?" Diabolo suggests. But because of his prominent belly that doesn't work. So he lies down, and Scarlett climbs up and straddles him with her back turned. It works a little better that way. Except Scarlett's scrofulous shoulders leave something to be desired.

Diabolo has the unpleasant impression of copulating with a little boy, or a little girl, so he has that droopy erection that always hurts Scarlett's feelings. But she's used to it.

Around noon the next day, Elias and Sandy wake up glued to each other. They finally manage to get up. Elias lends Sandy a shirt because she didn't take anything with her when she went out, and then it's really sexy, a girl in a guy's shirt that is too big for her. He empties the fridge to prepare a little breakfast Israeli style, with eggs and cheese, tomato-cucumber-hummus-and-tahini salad, a full pot of coffee, and a pitcher of orange juice. Enough to hold them till evening. Besides, they say the Jewish philosopher Maimonides recommended eating like a king in the morning, like a bourgeois at noon, and a beggar in the evening. Ever since he's been in Israel, Elias follows this diet exactly, but just in the morning: noon and evening, he often starves.

"How do you say 'cucumber' in Hebrew already?" asks Sandy.

"*Melafefone*," Elias answers, and Sandy can't help laughing because it sounds like a dirty word in French: "*Mets*—put—your lala in my foofoon," she says, dying of laughter, and that's all he needs to start over again.

She excites him with her slightest word. But she irritates him too. She's already irritating him. He screws her again even before she finishes her breakfast and sticks his prick in her mouth still full of salad. Only problem, somebody rings the bell at this very moment. Right in the middle of the bit. The landlady, of course! That old bitch bugging him again. Elias breaks off unwillingly, puts away his thing dripping with vinaigrette, and goes to open the door. My God, Juliette!

Juliette immediately glimpses Sandy on the couch covered with a little red wrap, and now her heart breaks into a thousand pieces. Oh no, not that! It's worse than a stabbing. Where can she go? What can she do? Why is life so unkind to her?

"It's not what you think! Not at all!" Elias says, still with a stiff erection.

Why did he make this poor girl come here? To humiliate her like this? But did he really make her come? Isn't she the one who announced she was coming to Tel Aviv? He should have said no, that was his mistake. But he didn't dare. Anyway, if everyone has his own version of the facts, one thing is certain: he's openly cheating on her, and she can't stand it.

Juliette immediately turns around. Elias tries to hold her back, but she pushes him away. She goes back down the rotten staircase. Sandy yells, "Elias, you coming back, or what?"

The worst of it all is that Elias didn't lose his hard-on for a second, despite all this drama.

# CHAPTER 4

Juliette walks around Florentin with tears in her eyes without knowing where to go, and lots of guys are tempted to console her on the way. Such a pretty girl! But she rebuffs them all, and to stop the little game she puts on her round Ray-Bans that make her even sexier but less accessible. She goes up Vital Street, where it's completely calm in the middle of the afternoon, unlike the evening, and finally stops at the terrace of Florentin 10 with a heavy heart. Sad and nauseous. Why did she leave her job at the museum and her apartment in Jeru? How idiotic! How could she have thought she'd go back to Elias without a crisis and without being disillusioned? How naive she was to believe in a happy household, *shalom bayit*, with a neurotic from the diaspora like him! And how long could she last in Tel Aviv with her five thousand shekels?

Manu only saw her two or three times a few months ago, but then he had both eyes. With gauze covering his right eye,

Marco Koskas

he obviously can't see as well. Romy really fucked him up, and he spent the night in the ophthalmic emergency room of Ichilov Hospital. The doctors weren't sure he'd get his eye back, but they did all they could. So he leaves the bar at Flo 10 to get closer, and once he's a yard away, there's no doubt about it. "Juliette?" he says in a low voice, because he sees she's in the middle of a crisis. She raises her head toward him, and as soon as she sees he has only one good eye, you'd think her own tragedy has yielded to his.

"Poor Manu," she says, distraught. "What happened to you?"

"Nothing, an accident at home, I got the cork of a bottle in my eye."

Juliette hugs him, moved to tears.

"They told me you escaped a stabbing attack, you must've been scared shitless."

"Sit down, sit down, please," she says, and without even answering his solicitude, she takes a handkerchief out of her purse to wipe the wound. Who knows why exactly. A compassionate reflex typical of her.

"No, no, I'm OK," Manu first says as he sits down. Then, looking at her with his only eye and seeing tears rolling down her cheeks, he says, "But you're crying . . . or am I seeing things?"

"Totally unimportant," she answers in a trembling voice.

"Don't say that. What's going on? It's because of Elias?"

24

She nods rapidly, sobbing. Manu hugs her. He's not supposed to have seen Sandy all over Elias the night before, right? He can act astonished. Ask questions. Play the guy who never heard about it.

"We-e-ll . . . he-he-here's what," she hiccups between sobs. "H-he was with another w-woman when I g-got there. B-but h-he knew I was coming! He did it on purpose, there's no other explanation . . . h-he's so destructive!"

Manu orders her a *café Affour* and gives her a Kleenex, stupidly repeating himself. Come on, come on, it'll be OK, don't think it's all over, blah blah blah. People can't really be consoled. So why try? Waste of time, it's well known. But on the other hand, how can you watch someone crying without trying to make them feel better? Especially such a pretty girl. He was struck by Juliette's fragility the first time he met her, but she controlled herself so well Manu was impressed. It was one evening in Jerusalem, and he thought she was really stoic with Elias, who was already mistreating her. Not a shout, not a tear. Proud, head high, a queenly bearing through it all. But that was in Jeru and that was back then. The poor darling isn't made of stone, after all. She must have a tolerance threshold, she can't always take everything stoically. In this kind of situation, it's better to change registers and ask concrete questions to help people who're hurting. Material life can assert itself over moods and emotions and change the atmosphere, Manu thinks.

"So you're going to go back to Jeru?"

"No-o-o, I c-came to live in Tel Aviv, and I don't have any-place to live in Jeru anymore. Except at my mother's, that is."

"So you need a place?"

"Well . . . yes," she confesses, sniffling.

"I have the key to an apartment in the Beans on Abarbanel Street."

"Whose is it?"

"It's in the brand-new buildings in front of my place. They look like beans. You can live there, OK?"

"Really? I can do that?"

"Well, yeah, the time for you to find something . . ."

"That's nice of you, Manu, but I don't feel I can live alone at this moment . . . I can't stay at your place, instead?"

"S-s-sure," Manu stammers, extremely embarrassed. "But you don't think . . . I mean, for Elias . . ."

"Please!" Juliette interrupts him, sobbing again. "It'll be a secret."

"Yeah, but just think of it . . . if Elias realizes you're living with me . . ."

"I'm just in no condition to remain alone. Try to under-stand me."

A beep from Manu's phone. Alert. A rocket was fired from Gaza. Hey, it's been a long time! After a year's pause, they're at it again. Since 2014, the alert hadn't sounded on the iPhone.

"Where'd it fall?" asks Juliette distractedly.

"Eshkol Regional Council, as usual," Manu answers, with a shrug.

"No kidding." Juliette smiles.

The alert works, too, to clear away her despondency. When there's something in the world greater than you are, war or faceless hatred, like Hamas's random bombardments of the southern towns, you forget yourself more easily. Still, for the knife intifada, we can't figure out what to do about it, and we can't find a solution.

At any rate, installing Juliette in his place and being Elias's best friend . . . he'd rather not think of the can of worms that's going to be, even if Juliette's stay will be as short as possible. For he'll have to lie. Lie about his eye, too, not only to Elias and Diabolo but also to other people, even to the waitresses at Flo 10—girls just out of the army, gorgeous and full of punch, who always want to know everything about his life. They ask all kinds of questions, so after a while they know everything except that he made porn movies for thirty full years. He would just give them one film like that, and it really cracked them up. Or else it didn't interest them at all. With them, the bullshit about the cork worked; Elias and Diabolo will ask more precise questions.

What's more, it's actually attempted rape, and on a member of the group, to boot. He could always say he just tried to grab her, but if she presses charges he'd be in the slammer, and fast. They don't kid around in the Promised Land. A young guy got ten years the week before, just for forcing a girl to kiss him. Even Katsav is rotting in prison in Ramla in a VIP cell for sexually assaulting his secretary, and he's the former president of the State of Israel. Israel is ultrademocratic, with a judicial system that has its hand on the trigger, with no pity for the powerful. That's the way it is. Manu had already been blind in one eye for a time when he was young, after an attack of uveitis. He tells himself he'll just pretend it's a new inflammation like that. It'll prevent questions . . .

# CHAPTER 5

As she arrives at his place, Juliette is struck by the beauty of the panorama, with the Yafo Mosque and the American church on the south side of the bank like two rival watchtowers over the Mediterranean. A new building went up these last few months on the north side, as if on purpose to block part of the sea view, but there's enough left for Manu to feel happy: every day he thanks the good Lord for giving him a landscape like this. Some mornings he does forget to express his gratitude, and then he feels guilty. He's afraid the good Lord will put him on His shit list.

While Juliette goes onto the balcony, Manu makes room for her things in the wardrobe. And gives her his room so she can be fully at ease. She protests a little for form's sake, but not exactly for form, either, because she has a half-hidden feeling of embarrassment at the idea that one night Manu could slip into bed with her. Whereas in other ways she trusts him completely. She has the tender feelings for him of an orphan for a father figure. But she also knows he has something hanging between his legs like all men, it was even his breadwinner for thirty years, and from one moment to another you never can tell with those things.

Manu is thinking of Romy. Why did he do that? What a dumbass thing to do! Could he even make up for such an act?

"She'll press charges!"

"Gimme a break!"

"I'm telling you!"

"Shit, they'll put me in the slammer!"

"Nah, I calmed her down with three thousand shekels. But they're costing me, your stupid escapades! You're lucky as hell she always thinks the wolf's at the door."

"You sure she won't press charges anyway?" Manu says.

"If you can spare two seconds, you might think of saying thanks!" Diabolo retorts, vaguely annoyed at Manu's ingratitude, before he hangs up.

"I've got to prepare," Elias announces suddenly.

"So?" Sandy asks.

"I need to concentrate."

"So?"

"So I have to be alone."

Sandy looks at him disgustedly. "After having a great time in my ass, is that it?"

30

He goes right under the shower in his tiny room, a space of a square yard with no wall, painted with orange-colored lime. Since he's been there, he's never even invested in a shower curtain, and Sandy gets splashed all over. She finally admits she's now one person too many there and takes off, insulting him as she leaves.

Try as he might to act cynical, Elias is disturbed by the pain he caused Juliette. He always gets into the same destructive spiral with women: he needs to hurt one to love another, to drive away the other to come back to the one before, as if there is a connection between all those women, and the wrong he did to the first is repaired by the good he did the next one, and so on. In fact, he's the connection—him and his anger.

As he gets dressed, he tells himself he'll call Juliette and apologize, but not right away. He doesn't want to owe her anything: let her expect nothing from him, even if he has a great feeling of tenderness for her. Not love, just tenderness. He calls Manu to tell him what happened when Juliette showed up at his place, but Manu, embarrassed by Juliette's hidden presence in his place, changes the subject to the state of his eye.

"How'd you do that?" Elias asks.

"Well . . . I was gonna string you along, but since Diabolo knows about it already, I might as well tell you the truth."

"Don't worry, we're just a little group," Elias says after hearing the story. "A microcosm, in fact! If Romy accepted the bread, she's not going to turn you in."

"You think so?"

"Sure . . . take it easy."

"What're you doing now?"

"Got a job interview at H24. I can come by later, if you want."

"Oh no! No!" he cries without thinking. "Let's meet, I dunno . . . let's meet at the Espresso Bar."

"OK, around six."

"What's FEMIS?" Marcel, the editor-in-chief and recruiter for Channel H24, asks, and Elias can't help pitying him instead of answering. Someone who doesn't even know the most elite film school in France.

"Anyway," Marcel follows up right away, "even if you passed the entrance exam, you didn't go there, right?"

"Right. I made my aliyah instead."

"And you know how to use a camera?"

"Of course."

Like all newsrooms, H24's is full of gorgeous girls, busy but smiling, and Elias tells himself he's fallen into the richest mine of women in all Israel. He spots four at first glance, particularly a certain Danielle Godmiche, a sublime Sephardi with a ponytail and a checked shirt, delicate as an artist's sketch. But the one he keeps coming back to is a blonde liana of twenty-four or twenty-five in white sneakers and a black lace miniskirt.

"So you're an engineer, and you want to be a reporter, a journalist?" the recruiter goes on.

"Well, yeah," Elias answers. "Miller was an office worker, and he became a writer at forty-two, you know."

"Miller? I thought he was a TV host."

"That one was a psychoanalyst first."

"An office worker or a psychoanalyst?" Marcel asks, confused.

The blonde gives him a sympathetic smile. Elias draws closer to her, leaving the ongoing conversation completely. But while he slips gently closer to her, Marcel keeps questioning him. A seduction maneuver, involuntary but totally successful, because the recruiter follows Elias like a shadow, standing just behind him, taking notes.

"My name's Olga," the pretty blonde says.

"You Ukrainian, or what?" Elias asks.

"No, no, my mother's the Ukrainian. But I grew up in Chambéry."

"When'd you get to Israel?"

"Two months ago. I started on a horse-racing channel in Paris, and they offered me an internship, so here I am."

"You interested in a trial job as a reporter at the Gaza border?" the recruiter asks, taking advantage of a pause in the conversation between the two turtledoves.

"Paying how much?"

"Eight thousand."

"I'm not risking my life for eight thousand bricks a month," Elias answers without turning around.

"We can go up to nine thousand if the trial is successful," adds Marcel.

"OK for ten thou'," Elias answers. "You draw up the contract, OK?"

A miraculous catch, this job interview, as Elias has killed two birds with one stone: a job and dinner the same evening with the miraculous Olga. Employed and in love! Really in love. Love at first sight, all the way. Only problem, he doesn't have a cent in his pocket and his credit card's maxed out. So on the way, he goes up to Manu's to borrow three hundred shekels. Knock knock knock. Manu motions Juliette to get into her hideout in the wardrobe closet, and Juliette obeys, slipping on the tile floor. It's really a pain, having to hide a girl in your own apartment.

Finally, Manu opens the door and says he would rather lend his friend five hundred shekels. It would be dumb to be too stingy when you're paying the check, right? It would be a little uncomfortable with his new conquest. For Elias really looks like he's in love! But he talks loudly, cries out that he loves her already, and Manu makes big gestures for him to lower his voice because Juliette must be able to hear everything.

Once Elias has left, Manu goes to get Juliette in her hiding place. He's extremely embarrassed, hoping she didn't hear anything or at least didn't understand exactly what Elias said.

"I'm sorry," she says as she gets out of the wardrobe. "If it's really too unpleasant for you, I can leave."

*Oh, good*, Manu tells himself, *sounds like she didn't hear a thing*. "No, no, just a lot of problems," he answers.

"See?" she says, biting her lips. "I'm just a weight on everybody. I'm one person too many on this earth." Tears are beginning to flow from her eyes again. "From the cradle on, I've been in the way, born out of wedlock."

"Stop it," says Manu, hugging her. "I'm very glad you're here."

"*Darling*," Diabolo says to Scarlett, using English, "you've been living at my place for twenty-four hours. You're going to be in the Guinness, I'm telling you!" Even if she doesn't catch the exact meaning of each word, she gets the strong impression she's reached the limits of her stay in Kerem.

"Well, hire me on, I'm Israeli after all. I can be useful," she answers in English, without emotion.

"OK, you want to do soccer?"

"OK by me. I want four thousand shekels a month," she demands.

And just to get rid of her, Diabolo agrees. His purse strings loosen more every day, but Diabolo remains optimistic. He's betting on a thousand subscriptions the very first year of his wire service. He expects a good hundred or so from French-speaking media, including national TV channels. And without going into detail, with the English version that's going to air soon, *Israel Breaking News* should also get the North American clientele and balance its books. Then, fortune or failure—we'll see . . .

# CHAPTER 6

Despite the coolness of the evening, Elias takes Olga to the balcony of the Hotel Montefiore. It has only two tables, and they're reserved months in advance. The brokers from Ramat Gan would sell their mothers to dine there with a girl. With its white tablecloths and silver settings, it's not the Israeli style at all, and even in Tel Aviv's trendy restaurants, it's not so common. Even the heaters set into console tables that cast the couples in a slightly pink glow are designed by fairy fingers. Everything is exquisitely refined. No chick could resist so many attentions. You're on the street but slightly above it and at the same time in an inaccessible ivory tower.

How did Elias manage to get one of two tables that same night? Who knows? At any rate, he put on a white Emile Lafaurie shirt, while Olga's wearing a pleated black skirt that goes down to the knees and lets you guess the graceful length of her legs. But she could put on a potato sack and she'd still be divinely pretty. As she already has two inches on Elias, she took it easy on the heels, wearing elegant plaited pumps, almost flat.

While he looks at her with a loving eye, he can't help wondering about the hidden resources women have when it comes to clothes. Olga must make eight thousand shekels a month max at H24, and she dresses like a princess twice a day! But she's not the only one. Juliette has the wardrobe of a diva, too, despite her wretched pay as an assistant at the museum in Jeru. In fact, all women have closets full, Elias tells himself. He always comes back to the famous Imelda Marcos, the Philippine dictator's widow, with her twelve hundred pairs of shoes. Or was it twelve thousand? Corrupt and venal as she was, there is nothing strange about her having a four-hundred-square-yard closet. But why that abundance with women who're basically broke? Collateral damage or compensation for penis envy? Who knows, Mose?

After dinner, two possibilities: either he brings her back to his pad on Levinsky Street and it's over, or he walks her back and tries to embed himself in her place. Olga lives at the corner of Yerushalaim and Salameh, at the edge of Yafo, an ordinary-looking building, butter-yellow facade and green shutters, except there's a pool on the roof. She told him this at dinner, and it's the kind of thing that makes Elias happy: it reinforces his idea that this country is both an antifatalist and anti-Puritan utopia. A pool on the roof in a country this dry, that takes some doing! Believing in your star with a direct challenge to climate theory. In those moments, the sacrifice Elias made in coming to live here when he could have made five thousand euros a month at Saint-Gobain seems totally justified.

But Olga makes him hang around for three days before granting him a first night at her place, as her grandmother was squatting in her bedroom during that time. A week later, Elias leaves his hole in the wall for an apartment at five thousand shekels a month, just across the street, still on Levinsky Street, on the eighth floor of a new high-rise. Diabolo lends him the deposit, practically without shilly-shallying. In those moments, his jaw goes up in a funny way, almost to his eyebrows, sort of like Popeye, and that means one thing: stop taking me for your banker, guys! On the other hand, he came to Tel Aviv with as much cash as the sand on Hilton Beach, and he doesn't mind people knowing it. He has no idea how to be discreet, Diabolo. Nor how to keep a low profile. Maybe he doesn't know the famous local joke: How do you become a millionaire in Israel? By being a millionaire when you get here.

And let's not forget, it's a country with communist origins, and like all such countries, it swung right into unbridled capitalism. With no second thoughts about it. But it's still a very small country, no bigger than three French *départements*, with barely eight and a half million inhabitants, and there aren't that many areas where you can make big bread. Number one: tech. Tied with real estate, which is flaming up like a crêpe suzette.

Even in Florentin, you find prices per square foot worthy of London. Now Diabolo is investing in the worst nag in the race: a quasi-activist press agency to try to squeeze out AFP, the big French news agency always ready to knock the State of Israel. But instead of starting small, he sees big right away. Crazy office space, insane hires.

The AFP correspondent finally gets bothered by it and quickly finds his pedigree. He gives him an appointment for an interview at Café Nina on Shabazi Street, and there he starts grilling him, but like a cop. He keeps pushing for the origin of the money at his disposal.

"It would be a bad idea to write about me, man," Diabolo warns him.

"What about freedom of expression?" the other retorts.

"What about my freedom to punch you in the nose?" Diabolo says, frowning.

Every time he goes straight, he runs into a guy who wants to sniff around in his past. And stay there. Forgiveness and redemption, never heard of it! On the other hand, you really do have to respect freedom of the press, transparency, and the whole nine yards. So everybody thinks they're within their rights, and the result of the contest is far from certain.

The AFP guy clears off fast, leaving Diabolo comfortably ensconced in his big body. Just afterward, here's the lovely Karen Besnainou coming to offer the services of her PR agency.

Diabolo goes to bed with her the same evening, but it doesn't go any further than that.

Now that Elias has started working as a reporter at H24 and Diabolo's a bigwig in the press (or almost), there's only Manu to recycle. He does get some subsidies from seasonal rentals, but he only has three apartments in his portfolio. What's more, even if Tel Aviv attracts tourists, since Operation Protective Edge in the summer of 2014 in Gaza, the vacancy rate has gone up. Add the low euro into the mix, and it's grown even more expensive. Too expensive. Either business has to start up again, or he has to fill out his portfolio and vary his offerings. But that means being in constant contact with the owners—mostly French—and that's beyond his powers. The only social milieu whose codes he knows is the world of X-rated movies. Elsewhere, he's adrift. Luckily the gays are faithful to Tel Aviv! That makes business thrive in the Beans on Abarbanel Street just across from him. As if his material survival, from porn to real estate, in all times and all latitudes, is always due to other people's libidos.

*I'm going to call it Jean-Pierre*, Elias says to himself as he picks up a little dying cat from under a car parked on Herzl Street.

"What about the salary?" Juliette shyly asks the owner of Gallery Moins de Mille just down from Manu's place with its back against the slums.

Normally an area like this would have been razed to make room for a little park. But since its inhabitants have gone through all kinds of maneuvers to block it, it's still in limbo. Shows you people hang on to the little they have, even if it's ugly and unhealthy. And then city planning is too geometric and rigid. For example, since they've finished the four Beans on Abarbanel Street, everybody agrees they should leave the slums alone, in the last analysis, and not necessarily destroy everything to make a park. By preserving that habitat, they'd create a kind of contrast between the old and the new, all the more so as there are a lot of little trades that are plied under those corrugated metal roofs. Furniture makers, framers, upholsterers, and now the Moins de Mille gallery. In short, they should reboot the city plan for the neighborhood.

"Let's say I can give you twenty-five hundred shekels a month part time," the gallery owner says.

"That's not much," Juliette answers, looking around at this odd place, where the paintings are arranged any old way.

"But you'll have a lot of responsibility," he adds. "I'm counting on you to reorganize things, OK? I like to hunt around for antiques and stuff, and I have an eye, but I need someone who has a sense of space and public relations."

"OK for twenty-five hundred, but just three afternoons a week," Juliette proposes, looking for her phone. It's in the palm of her hand, as it has been since the knife attack.

"I don't like cats, Elias darling. I'm allergic," Olga confesses.

"All right, I'll put it back in the street."

"No, no, he's so cute. Try to give him to someone."

# CHAPTER 7

In the two weeks since she got to Tel Aviv, Juliette has cried a lot, felt sorry for herself, and complained. A contradictory mixture of hope and despair is beginning to grow in her mind. She thinks she can see Elias coming back to her, and she's even ready to forgive his transgression. On the other hand, she doesn't believe he'll really come back. Up to now, she's suffered the usual torment of dupes. What's new is her need to obtain reparation. She feels Elias owes her something, without knowing exactly what. Manu made her admit she decided to live in Tel Aviv on her own, not because Elias asked her to, but still. She expects reparations.

She sent him message after message, and he never answered. So one night she goes back to see him, but Elias has moved! What's more, without telling her! Why such cruelty? Does she mean so little to him? And Manu—why didn't he tell her anything, he who's so protective of her? She bites her lips, but the sobs squeeze her like a vise.

"Tell me where he's living, Manu . . . please."

"Why, Juliette? How would that help you?"

"It's my right, Manu! I have a right to know!"

"Still on Levinsky Street," Manu finally answers, with a sigh.

"That's not true, I went there!"

"But in another building . . ."

"Alone?"

"No."

"Who is that girl, Manu? What's her name? Is she the one I found him with?" she asks, half smothering a sob.

"No," Manu answers, embarrassed. "It's not her."

"So who is it?" Juliette yelps in despair.

"What's the use of all these questions, Juliette?"

"Come on, Manu, you have to understand me, I need to know! It's killing me! I want to meet her!"

"Why?"

Good question. Does Olga have anything to do with Juliette's misfortune? She doesn't even know she exists, since Elias didn't tell her about their relationship. Besides, the fact that they work together at H24 gives them another, much more important problem: Announce it, or be discreet? Elias is so in love with Olga he'd shout it from the rooftops. Olga is more prudent. There's so much jealousy in a TV station. Luckily,

Elias is always out in the field and Olga's in the studios. That way they have less contact during the day and won't give themselves away by a gesture or a word. But Tel Aviv is a small place. In the French community you can hear someone sneezing for miles around. Rumors fly quickly too. And then you can easily bump into someone on the street who works in TV, so that creates another connection with the stars of the small screen. Sometimes that proximity is unbearable. In Par Derrière, the restaurant on King George Street, it's like eating with the TV on when there's Danielle Godmiche at the table next to you.

What's more, Elias is bored as hell at the Gaza border. Too calm. Deadly calm, in fact. Since the ceasefire of August 14, 2014, the front totally cooled off. In ten days, all Elias covered was the story of a little Gaza girl of eight who was transported to the Israeli hospital of Be'er Sheva for a heart operation. He didn't put the necessary pathos into it so they had to jazz it up to get it on TV, and that didn't sit well with Elias.

"You're not gonna tell me what montage is!"

"It's not the movies, it's TV," editor-in-chief Marcel fires back, "and you better get used to it!"

Olga followed this from afar, biting her lip. Even though she's ten years younger than he is, she knows the codes of a TV channel better than he does. Rule number one: Never confront someone directly. Everything behind the back. All base deeds on the q.t.; Elias is the opposite. He enjoys this kind of conflict. He gets off on it.

So he asks either to go back to the newsroom or to cover Judea and Samaria, and Marcel proposes a correspondent in . . . Jenin, on the West Bank. You take your life in your hands. With his Sephardic face, Elias wouldn't have time to put a foot on the ground before he'd be lynched. Even with an Arab cameraman, it'd be scary as hell. So he remains sagely at the Gaza border, taking notes.

In the futuristic novel he dreams of writing, the main character will be Amos Kirzenbaum, an Israeli-like des Esseintes in Huysmans's *Against the Grain*, a rich aesthete who'll be the last Jew in Tel Aviv after the disappearance of the Jewish state. A *uchronia*, a waking nightmare.

Every other day he comes back to Tel Aviv and spends the night with Olga. But they sleep at her place because Olga still can't stand the little cat he adopted.

"Just the time he needs to recover, and I'll find him a host family," Elias promises. He goes to see Manu to ask him to adopt Jean-Pierre, and Manu starts to panic because he opened the door without thinking about his new roommate, Juliette. Too late, Elias is there with Jean-Pierre in his jacket. Now, Juliette happens to be out, and it's even worse than if she were there, because she may return at any moment. Manu thinks of texting her, telling her not to come back for a little while, but he tells himself she'd sense that Elias was there and she'd zip right back.

In short, it's at that unusual moment of panic that Manu agrees to adopt Jean-Pierre, the cat—Manu, who never could stand cats. Juliette's the opposite. She loves them and immediately gets a crush on the kitty. If only she knew it was Elias's cat. Manu told her he found it in the street. She takes care of it lovingly, and it's quite touching to see her give it so much love. In fact, Manu thinks she's right to want kids, she'd make a wonderful mom—an excellent nurse, too, as she takes such good care of his wounded eye. Eye lotion twice a day, pomade, and a new dressing. She does this gently, delicately, very tenderly. She is really made to love. And to give. Manu imagines that if she began to hate someone with the same devotion, she could become a criminal. With devoted people, it can easily swing. They need the absolute, those people. They don't know how to hold off, to play for time. And put things in perspective. Devoted people are potential criminals, that's all there is to it.

But there is a certain embarrassment between them: she never looks Manu in the eye. She always turns her head. Yes, looking a man straight in the eye. Well, it's troubling. It's too intimate. She only really looks Manu in the eye when she takes care of him, when he's in such a state of dependence that there could be no sexual connection between them. It's only in porn that the nurse finds the patient exciting, and God knows how many movies Manu made with Taba Cash disguised as a nymphomaniac nurse! But there's nothing exciting about a sick guy. Nor woman, in fact. It arouses compassion, not passion. And yet, no one can deny that there's something favorable to sex in the caregiver/cared-for relationship.

Besides, between Manu and Juliette, that's not the only connection that might arouse the desire for sex. When he glimpses her coming out of the bathroom naked, he thinks of it. And she does, too, very furtively, since she's sleeping in his bed. She's even the one who thinks of it most often, although she immediately rejects the thought as indecent. She can't wait to find her own place. Every day, she goes to visit apartments, but it's always too expensive or too small or too ugly. And then she doesn't feel able to live alone, for the moment . . .

"I'm leaving to cover a story for a week," Olga announces.

"Where?" Elias asks.

"In Gérardmer, in the Vosges. There's a film festival."

"But that's absurd! Why not me? I got into FEMIS, for godsake. I know something about movies."

"Well, yeah, I know. You want me to turn it down?"

"No, no, but still . . ."

It's the first time she sees him frustrated, and that's a strong contrast with the magnetism he usually has. All of a sudden, his lips are pinched and the whites of his eyes turn whiter than white. The cinema is such a source of frustration! Even if Elias gave up FEMIS, he still hopes to succeed in making a film some-day; everything brings him back to the sacrifice he made when he came to Israel and reconnects him to his initial anger at the whole world. Olga's the opposite. As she never encountered the slightest vexation in her young life, she has no way of taking the measure of the extent of his inner anger, which is deep, and old. Ancestral, even. After a few hours it goes away, of course. But Olga found the change spectacular, and she's leaving the next day for Gérardmer with that strange impression in her mind.

Alone with his camera at the Gaza border, Elias smokes cigarette after cigarette, waiting for something to happen. He needs money to give Olga a splendid gift, impress her, and materialize that love in a symbolic object. A ring—that would be ideal. But where can he find the bread? He already owes Diabolo five thousand shekels and five hundred to Manu.

He leaves his post and goes driving through the Negev at random, filming the rocky landscape of that mineral desert. All that beauty inspires the filmmaker and writer that lie dormant within him. He imagines a Western with Patrick Bruel running a falafel stand in this setting—that would be a ball—and Lee Van Cleef as a sinister visitor who doesn't take his eyes off him. Except Lee Van Cleef is dead, and there's no great actor with an unsettling face anymore. Then Elias starts making financial calculations, and the *yetzer hara*, as they say in Hebrew, slips into his imagination—the inclination for evil, you might say. Dirty tricks go through his mind and stick there. The station's four-wheel drive must still be worth a hundred thousand shekels. It's a rather old-model Subaru. Why not try to sell it and claim it was stolen?

He knows there's a gang of slightly criminal Bedouins near Mitzpe Ramon. They live on a rock from which there's an amazing view over the valley. He spends the night there out in the open, sending texts full of love to his beauty. Toward dawn, two Bedouins draw near. Elias starts the negotiations in Hebrew, and the deal is concluded over a cup of scalding tea under the tent: fifty thousand shekels in two installments, twenty-five thou' up front and the rest a month later—with the papers for the vehicle.

Now the equation is simple: Either he claims he was attacked by these Bedouins and they stole his car in exchange for his life. Then there'd necessarily be a police investigation. It would be his word against theirs. Or . . . or nothing. The unknown in this equation is when the truth will come out.

He goes back to Tel Aviv by bus, with twenty-five thousand shekels in his pocket. On the way, he finally gets a text from Olga: *Real happy to be back to snow and France. Kisses.* Not the great declaration he was waiting for, and this bugs him. Does she miss him so little? And then Marcel calls him to commission a story on the new rocket that fell on a vacant lot near Sha'ar HaNegev, but he doesn't answer. Marcel repeats his request by text this time, and Elias texts back that his camera is broken. *Come back and get good equipment*, Marcel answers obligingly. Before going back to H24, Elias makes a detour by Kerem HaTeimanim to explain his situation.

"No two ways about it," Diabolo answers unhesitatingly. "Gotta get the wheels back."

"But how?"

"I'll take care of it."

"When?"

"Tonight, man! But you're starting to be a real pain in the ass with your problems, Elias!" Diabolo says. "Give me two thou' for the kitty . . ." (A communal cash depot Diabolo invented to finance future parties and, incidentally, help new French immigrants.)

"Should I come with you?" Elias asks.

"You off your rocker, or what? Find yourself something to do instead, with a witness."

"Yoni! You're not in Jeru anymore?" Juliette exclaims as she walks by the sidewalk café of Florentin 10. They exchange affectionate kisses, give each other the well-known Israeli hug, and Juliette sits down with him.

"I've been here for six months already. All my buddies are here," Yoni answers, adjusting his yarmulke.

"What'll you have?"

"A *café Affour*. How about Maia? Where is she?"

"At home. We have an apartment on Matalon. So you're not in Jeru anymore either?"

"Well, no, I . . . came . . . how can I say this? I came for . . . you know, I have a boyfriend, but, OK, so I . . . I didn't see him yet . . ." And tears start flowing down Juliette's cheeks, so Yoni gives her an affectionate squeeze on the wrist.

"Your boyfriend is Elias, right?"

"Yes, yes. You know him?"

"Yeah, sure. We went through our Hebrew immersion classes together."

"Oh, I see . . ."

"I'll talk to him."

"No way!" she retorts. "He owes me an explanation. I want him to admit he did me wrong. You know where I can find him?"

The waitress brings over Yoni's breakfast: sausages, sautéed potatoes, yogurt with cereal, and cream cheese. Juliette watches Yoni eat without daring to tell him that it isn't very kosher. Neither the sausage nor the mix of meat and dairy. Well, he has a right to do that, but then, why the yarmulke?

"I heard he's working at H24," Yoni finally consents to tell her.

"The French channel?" Juliette says, getting up already.

At the entrance to H24, security stops Juliette. No pass, no H24 ID. But she asks the guy to call the editor-in-chief, and a few minutes later, Marcel arrives with his two phones screwed into his ears.

"Elias Benzaquen?" he says. "He's our correspondent at the Gaza border. He's never here."

"When's he coming back?" Juliette asks with a repressed sob, and Marcel realizes that a heavy drama is making a knot in this gorgeous young woman's throat. It confirms Elias is a lady-killer, but part of his job is also not to give in to the swarms of pretty girls who're constantly after him.

"That depends on events, I can't tell you when, exactly," he says as he leaves, a purely professional reflex.

At least Juliette now knows Elias isn't permanently in Tel Aviv. She leaves H24 and goes to sit down on the dock, as the offices of the channel are right on the port of Yafo. Her thoughts wander as she watches the sea, so different from what it is in Tel Aviv, although the two places are right next to each other. In Yafo, it's a Caribbean blue and so clear it makes you feel like plunging in—even drowning in it. You'd think it was a commercial for scuba diving. Seen from Yafo, the Tel Aviv beach takes on another dimension and makes you think of those huge seaside resorts in Florida, lined with tall buildings. Unlike Tel Aviv, there are also many Arabs out with their families in the port of Yafo, with the women wrapped in cloth like mummies and the men looking like sailors.

Juliette sits there, telling herself maybe she could get a job at H24. She'd be exactly where she'd have to be to collar Elias. But she probably doesn't have the required competences, even though she's fluent in Hebrew, English, and French. And then there's the impression she left on Marcel, a poor unhappy woman—not exactly the best CV.

# CHAPTER 8

When it gets out of Mitzpe Ramon, the Fiat 500 enters a narrow trail that winds up the flank of the hill, and Diabolo's imposing form bounces up and down on the driver's seat as if he were on a trampoline. According to the map Elias made him, you've got to trek like that for a little under a mile before you hit the Bedouin encampment. Down from the camp, a camel tethered to a stake shows you're almost there. Then there are only three hundred yards to go, but on foot. There, Diabolo turns off the ignition. The twilight is still too light for him to intervene. As he waits for night to fall, he lights up a Cohiba and breathes out the biggest cloud of smoke you can get from a Havana cigar. Next to him, Jonathan Simsen gets a huge whiff right in the nose but doesn't complain, even though he's forbidden to open the windows so as not to alert a possible watchdog.

Once they can't see at all, Diabolo gives Jonathan his orders: "You're going to go back down toward Mitzpe Ramon and wait for me at the end of the path. You got to manage to drive without turning on the lights. If I'm not back in two hours, come back up here. OK?"

Diabolo painfully extricates himself from the car, cursing himself for not renting a vehicle better adapted to his corpulence. But he got it for practically nothing. Hardly a thousand shekels a month! While Jonathan maneuvers in the darkness, Diabolo slips toward a meager, vacillating gleam farther off, trusting the echo of a woman's voice to guide him.

Prudently, he approaches the Bedouins' camp: two tents. Luckily, no dog to reveal his presence by barking. He sees at a glance that two men and two women live there with a swarm of children. The four-wheel drive must be hidden between the two tents, but Diabolo can't see it yet.

Once the kerosene lamp is out in the first tent, he goes ahead. But his first step crunches too much on the stony ground. So he delays again, and without putting one step right after another, it takes him over five minutes to reach the car, which is only twenty yards away.

When Diabolo sees that the vehicle is there between the two tents, he breathes a sigh of relief. He takes a Ping-Pong ball out of his pocket. He'd already carefully cut out one part of it like a soft-boiled egg, and now he slaps it against the lock of the door and crushes it with a sharp blow of his palm. It works! An old gypsy trick he learned in the prison of Fresnes. The lock opens through the push of compressed air. Things start going less well once he starts up the engine. Right away, one disheveled Bedouin surges out of the tent and then the other, armed with a long club. Then Diabolo takes more direct action. He throws the four-wheel drive into reverse and crashes headlong into one of them, while the second man throws himself at the door to try to climb into the car. Diabolo has to give him two hard shots with his elbow to neutralize him. His assailant falls back in his turn, and the way is finally clear. Diabolo stamps down the accelerator and succeeds in escaping with the four-wheel drive.

Dammit! Why must he always find himself in these rotten situations? Always on the margins and always in the red zone. Sure, out of friendship for Elias. But when he made his aliyah, he'd sworn to himself all that was over and done with. And yet it's beginning again. He's so sick of throwing out punches! At the same time, let's be honest, it's fun. Poor Diabolo, he's so bored in normal life. He has so many ideas for making money, so many women to screw, so many parties to give, so many cigars to smoke. The days are too short and the temptations too great. Besides, it's strange for a hedonist like him to take other people's problems so seriously. But that's the way he is. A real old-time hood, with balls and a soul. A head, too, Diabolo. You wouldn't think it, but he has a degree in history. He tried to defend his doctoral dissertation twice, but no luck, the cops were holding him for questioning on both occasions. Otherwise he'd have a PhD in medieval history.

Elias can thank heaven for having a friend who gets him out of a real jam and takes all the risks. Once he's reimbursed the deposit on the apartment, he still needs eighteen thousand shekels for Olga's ring. That should go all right, except that news from his darling is so rare Elias has a feeling of foreboding. One text in four days. What if this great love between him and Olga isn't as mutual as all that? Oh, come on! He drives the idea out of his mind and goes into a jeweler's on Dizengoff Avenue at the corner of Ben Gurion. The saleslady in an elegant, tight-fitting dark suit shows him wonders, and he feels like buying everything—and screwing her, too, but that's his bad instincts again, his *yetzer hara*. And yet she's old, with as much makeup on as a stolen car. But there you are, it's Elias's baser instincts at work.

He finally decides on a finely chiseled gold bracelet because the symbolism of the ring does seem a bit too strong for such a recent relationship. But for the cash payment, after locking the entrance to the shop, the saleslady asks him to follow her into the back office. Once they're alone, Elias slowly takes the money out of his pocket, looking the jeweler in the eyes for a long time. She has a little embarrassed smile, and Elias puts the stack of bills on the table with great precaution. While she's recounting, he comes up to her and flattens himself against her hips. She doesn't move. Then he puts his hand under her skirt, and she sighs softly while he strokes her thighs. She keeps counting the bills for a few moments, but she finally gives out a heavy groan when he stuffs two fingers into her. "Come back and see me often," she murmurs to him in Hebrew before he leaves the shop.

# CHAPTER 9

When he reaches H24's parking lot, he rips out a random valve in the engine to make the four-wheel drive unusable. That way, he'll go back to the Gaza border with another vehicle, in case the Bedouins want to find him and take their revenge. Then he brings back his supposedly malfunctioning camera to the equipment office. Next he goes to see Marcel, who immediately tells him about Juliette's visit.

"I hope you didn't give her my address!"

"Hey, I'm not crazy," Marcel answers soberly. "Any news from Olga?"

"Why would I have news of Olga?"

"Everybody knows you're together."

Elias takes it in stride, waits a moment, and then starts up again as if nothing had happened.

"I also need another car, Marcel. Mine broke down."

"The car, too?"

"Afraid so. Sand's not great for the motor."

"Did you go to the garage?"

"Yeah, but there's nothing available."

So Elias hangs around the newsroom, waiting to get a new vehicle. He sits down at Olga's desk for a moment, thinking of the first magical moments of their meeting, when she couldn't concentrate on her screen anymore and she only had eyes for him. That was hardly two weeks ago.

He calls Manu to pay him back, and they set up a meeting at the Café Français on Rothschild Boulevard. It used to be the library of the French Institute. But there were a lot fewer people there. Now it's always full. It is *the* place to be in Tel Aviv, the spot where all the bourgeois bohemians want to be seen.

"You know Juliette's in Tel Aviv?"

"Uh . . . well, sort of, but no, not really, why?" Manu stammers.

"It worries me, she's following me. Dunno who told her I was working at H24. Seems she came by this morning. Crazy, right?"

"Yes, it's strange," Manu says, embarrassed and looking away.

"Hey, here's your five hundred bucks," Elias says, handing over some bills. "If you see her, not a word about me, OK?"

"Of course!"

Manu returns to Florentin determined to press Juliette to find her own place. She's already started working three mornings a week at the Moins de Mille gallery, and that gives her a little income but not enough to pay rent. The cheapest studio apartment in Florentin is four thousand shekels a month. A little less than a thousand euros since the sharp drop in the European currency, and that makes it still more for her. In the slum just next to the brand-new Beans, you can find something less expensive, but they're sad dwellings with no AC and sometimes no window. Since you live outside a lot in Tel Aviv, it's less serious than in a colder country, but it's still hard to live in them.

Now Manu is even more eager for her to move, because it really weighs on him to lie to Elias, but on the other hand he's also starting to like her presence in his apartment. She's so sweet and gentle. A little melancholy but very sweet, and truly friendly. In fact, she arrived at the best possible moment in Manu's life: after his horrible night with Romy. Without Juliette he would have had to treat his eye alone, for example, and that would have been really depressing. And then she's beginning to look him in both eyes, or rather in one eye, outside of the moments when she's changing his dressing, and something very tender is connecting them. Having breakfast together on the balcony is a great pleasure, he must admit: a moment for lovers, if truth be told. But he's thirty years older than she is with no advantages and no prospects, so let's not get carried away here.

The most touching thing is her unbelievable attachment to Jean-Pierre, the cat. He has become her cat, and Manu promised she can take him with her when she has her own apartment. Sometimes he longs to tell her it's Elias's cat, if only to see her reaction. It might be funny. She'd be capable of seeing a sign of fate in that, she's so fragile. Well, no. Might as well let her love the animal without bothering her.

In Florentin, Jean-Pierre is the favorite cat, because the cats run wild in the neighborhood, like in the rest of Tel Aviv. Devoted neighbors feed them, but they adore dogs. You have to see the girls in Florentin pick up their dogs' turds with an abnegation they'd probably never have for a guy. So those animals think they can do anything at all. The dogs yap at each other from one sidewalk to another and spread out like doormats at the entrance to restaurants. It's all about them. On Florentin Street, there are two shops devoted to their needs: air-conditioned kennels, plastic bones, dog food with added vitamins, toothpicks for poodles. At least cats get along fine on their own, without bugging anybody. Moreover, the difference in condition between cats and dogs in Tel Aviv makes you think of an animal representation of the gap between Sephardim and Ashkenazim in Israel, although with the arrival of the French, Sephardim are now becoming the privileged part of society. They invest, they speculate, they set up bakeries, call centers, hip restaurants, and a bunch of things Israelis love, like that Café Français on Rothschild Boulevard. At some future time, Tel Aviv will be a French city.

# CHAPTER 10

"I didn't think I'd miss you so little, only, there you are . . ." Olga begins, without opening the purple velvet case Elias set before her. "I don't want to lie to you, Elias. I'm not really in love with you."

"I think I'm gonna die," Elias mumbles, with his head down.

"Don't say that, I mean, we didn't . . . look, we barely had two weeks together. It's not exactly . . . let's stay friends. We work at the same place, after all."

"I'm gonna die," he repeats stubbornly, pushing the case containing the bracelet toward her. That doesn't persuade her to open it any more than when he put it in front of her.

She's so embarrassed by their conflicting emotions! And although she doesn't want to let herself be moved by pity, Elias's incredible distress does catch her unprepared. Never would she have thought he'd be so upset. She was even sure he'd already be with another girl when she got back from Gérardmer. Maybe she's had the wrong idea about him? Maybe he's not a cynical seducer but an ultrasensitive guy? Fragile, even? With men, she never knows what is pure show and what's truly driving them. But she knows when someone makes her vibrate and when those vibrations fade away. And that's how it is with Elias.

So she gets up delicately, as if to disappear without making a sound, almost sliding, but she sees Elias crying his eyes out and that holds her back for a few moments. Just a few moments. She quickly caresses his hair, and then she clears out.

The sky fell on his head, poor Elias. And not just the sky. The planets and the stars, too, especially his lucky star with girls since it's the first time one has ever left him.

The first mad love of his life flies off, and here he is like a schmuck on the sidewalk of the Café Français, the worst spot in Tel Aviv to burst into tears. The day is not over, but it already seems interminable to him, and he can't see how to get through tomorrow under these conditions, much less survive for a few days. That's typical of what you feel after an unhappy love affair: it prevents you from moving forward, it nails you to the spot and crucifies you. All Elias wants is to die. He needs a support, a charitable hand. It's too hard to face the nothingness that's coming in. What meaning does his life have now? He'd dreamed of a future with Olga. A pretty house in Yafo, the garden, the kids, the dog.

"Got it, Elias, there's a car available. You coming to get it? I need someone at the border."

"She left me, Marcel!" Elias howls. "Olga dropped me! You brought me bad luck, you bastard! I don't give a shit about Gaza! I'm gonna die, shit, I'm gonna die!" He sobs into the phone.

"Where are you?"

"I don't even know. In the street."

"Get a grip on yourself, Elias! I'm begging you, tell me where you are!"

"I wanna die!" Elias is still bellowing, in a quavering voice. "I don't wanna live any mo-o-o-re!"

"I'm coming!" says Manu.

"I'm coming!" says Diabolo, in turn.

They find Elias right in Bnei Brak, sitting on a park bench in the neighborhood of the nuts in black—and for good reason, because in that area you can't find a single café. The stores are hideous, the stands would make any customer flee, you'd think you were on the outskirts of Lahore if it weren't for the clear laughter of adorable high school girls in pleated skirts at the bus stops.

"I've got my dose of ugly crap for today," Diabolo decides as he forces Elias to get into the Fiat 500.

"I wanna die!" Elias howls, resisting.

"OK, but not here," Manu retorts, helping Diabolo push him inside.

They start off.

"All that for a chick of twenty-five," mumbles Diabolo crossly, lighting up a Cohiba.

"She really threw you out?" Manu asks, thinking maybe that might be good for Juliette. Besides, should he announce it to Juliette? After all, if Elias would go back to her after this, that would help him out. It would bother him, too, because he's becoming more attached to Juliette. So what should he do? A dilemma, for two blondes!

"Shit, how'm I gonna live without her?" Elias is still sobbing. "You can't understand how much I love her! I don't want anyone else! I wanna di-i-i-e!"

"Oh, shut up!"

They go back under pouring rain to spend an all-guys night in Kerem. Water is beginning to rush down the sloping streets and make ponds at the intersections. Not a soul on the Tayelet, and the beach cafés have all packed up their outdoor chairs and tables. It thunders over the city like an F-16 going Mach 2. It's spectacular to watch, that sky striped with flashes of lightning—a bit apocalyptic, too, but that's Tel Aviv in winter. Diabolo heats up the oven and in no time at all comes out with a chicken *basquaise* with tiny lima beans. They don't even leave a bone.

"I wanna di-i-i-e!" Elias yells again over dessert.

# CHAPTER 11

Juliette is somewhat apprehensive as she walks to the address listed in the ad. It's painful to go back there. Bad memories come flooding in, but she finally overcomes those unpleasant thoughts because the rent is very low and also because the landlady is a darling Yiddish mama: "I'd rather have a girl like you than the tenant who used to be here—a guy with his fly open all the time! Keep the deposit for your wedding dress," she adds, kissing her like good bread. "A beautiful blonde like you still unmarried? The good Lord's gone crazy!"

Juliette signs the one-year renewable lease at three thousand shekels a month, and now she's ready to settle in with Elias's old cat in Elias's old furnished room on Levinsky Street, just across the street from the high-rise where Elias is now living.

She calls her mother immediately to tell her the good news, for it really is good news to have finally found a place to live.

"So you're living with Elias?" Sandrine asks.

"Uh, yes . . . I mean, no . . . well, not with him directly but in this place . . . with Jean-Pierre," Juliette stammers.

"Jean-Pierre? Who is this boy?"

"I'll explain it to you later."

"Explain it to me now, darling."

"I can't, Mom, my battery's almost dead. Love you, Mom." And she hangs up.

Since she's been in Tel Aviv, Juliette has always used this stratagem to dodge questions from her mother and avoid worrying her. Sandrine is such a fragile woman. She runs back down Abarbanel Street to tell Manu she's finally going to free up his bedroom and clear out.

"You don't even have a bed," he points out.

"No problem, I'll buy a foam mattress on Herzl Street. They have some cheap ones."

"You're not going to repaint the place before you move in? It was pretty grotty when Elias was there."

"The landlady repainted. It's spotless."

"At least wait till your stuff comes in from Jeru."

"No, no, I'm ready to be in my own place."

"Well, at least stay tonight."

"No, Manu, I'm telling you, I've squatted here long enough."

"OK. But I'm going to miss you. I like you being here," he declares, taking her in his arms.

She lets him, but she doesn't know how to react to this sudden surge of affection. Normally, you don't get a hard-on when you hug a friend. Now, she can feel the erection taking shape in his jeans, a big stick, in fact. But she doesn't dare push him away either. She just hopes he's not going to take advantage of the situation—try to kiss her, for example.

"Just a kiss," Manu whispers, searching for her mouth.

"Stop, please, Manu, stop it . . . we have . . . I mean, you could be my father . . ."

"I like you, Juliette."

"Don't say that, please, Manu," she begs, while he squeezes her a little harder and his hand slips down her dress and pushes into the cloth, between her buttocks.

She knees him in the groin, and he lets go of her fast, collapsing onto the couch, writhing in pain.

"Oh, I'm sorry, Manu, forgive me, please forgive me," she implores, falling at his feet. "I didn't want to . . . but understand me . . . wait, I'll get you a glass of water . . . oh, God, what have I done!"

She runs to the fridge and takes out a bottle of Ein Gedi, takes a glass from the cupboard, and comes back to give Manu a drink. He's all hunched up on the couch.

"Drink, Manu, please! Drink, you'll see, that'll do you good," she begs, holding out the glass, which he doesn't take. "Breathe! Breathe in, it'll go away."

"Ow! Oh, oh!" Manu groans. "Oh, God! I never hurt so much in my life . . . ohhh . . . I'm gonna die."

"Forgive me. I didn't know what else to do," Juliette stammers out.

"I'm gonna go to the hospital, ow, oh, oh."

Then Juliette sets the glass of water down on the low table and slides her hand slowly up his thigh to the fly and methodically unbuttons it. "Let me do this," she whispers, slipping her hand delicately inside his pants. Little by little Manu relaxes, the pain goes away through her magical caress, and Juliette diligently sucks him to calm it completely. Then she gets up.

"There, Manu, I hope we're even now."

"I'm so sorry, Juliette, I swear I wasn't faking and then—"

"And then nothing," she cuts him off. "I'm going to pack my things, and you're going to forget what happened. OK?"

"Do take a pair of sheets," Manu says, with some embarrassment, as he closes his pants.

"Thanks. It's still OK for me to take Jean-Pierre with me, right?"

"Of course, of course, he's your cat now."

"Where's Jean-Pierre?" asks Elias as he comes into Manu's apartment the next day, wearing a cap and fatigues a little too big for him. But above all, his eyes are red, continually red. All he does since Olga left is cry. So Marcel granted him a few days off, and he wanders from café to café like a lost soul. He hasn't returned to Levinsky Street to sleep, and he hasn't swallowed anything, either, aside from wine and coffee. He's visibly melting away, but he feels better on an empty stomach. He fasted so much, before.

"Jean-Pierre?" Manu says, caught off guard. "I dunno, he must be out roaming around."

"Where the hell can he roam? You live on the fifth floor."

"Maybe at the neighbors'? He must've gone by the balcony."

"Can you check, please? I'd like to get him back. At least *he* won't drop me."

Manu does a quick round trip to the neighbors' and comes back relieved. "Nobody home."

# Chapter 12

The next day, Elias gets back on the road to Gaza in another four-wheel drive, this one painted with the station's colors—a brand-new Toyota, equipped with a fridge and a Nespresso machine. Marvelously kitted out for a road trip. On the way, he gets a call from Juliette, who wants to tell him she took his apartment on Levinsky Street, but he doesn't answer, and she hangs up without leaving a message. That gets him into a very odd state—let's say a certain sexual excitement—which doesn't go very well with his suffering, because normally one drives out the other. Now, one may have driven out the other, but the other returns through the back door. It's not that they're in a tie inside his heart, far from it, but he wouldn't mind going to bed with Juliette again because that affair has left him with the taste of something unfinished.

Maybe he'll go see her when he gets back from Gaza. Hey, besides, where could she be living in Tel Aviv? It's the first time he asks himself the question. Then Olga takes over his thoughts again, and once more, he starts crying.

He goes to the Golani unit at the Nahal Oz kibbutz to report his return and then goes to park the car at the foot of the artificial dune they built facing Gaza. After four days of storms, the sun has returned, but those torrential rains have transformed the landscape. The stony countryside has given way to an incongruous green and the dune is now a grassy hill, already dotted with poppies.

A message from Marcel arrives right away, asking for a story on the collapse of Hamas's tunnels in Gaza, precisely because of the bad weather. Elias calls his contact in the Shin Bet, who confirms the info. He climbs to the top of the dune with his camera and takes a few wide shots of the fence. An interview on FaceTime with the Golani Brigade unit's commander and archival footage of the tunnels, and he'll have enough to produce a story in a couple of minutes.

That distracts him from his torment somewhat, but he constantly wipes his eyes as he works, because his tears flow even without him noticing it. After a few shoulder shots, he sits down in the back of the four-wheel drive for the FaceTime interview, and the picture of the Golani unit's commander appears on the screen.

"Hello, Illan. Sorry to bother you, but could you give me a few words about the collapse of the tunnels?" Elias asks in Hebrew.

"You crying, or what?" Illan says.

"No, just conjunctivitis."

"According to our info," the officer says, "there were a lot of cave-ins, yes, and . . ."

At that moment, the side door of the car swings open, and Elias feels himself being snatched up and pulled outside and thrown to the ground. Dammit, the two Bedouins—they found him! Must be the "Arab telephone"—the grapevine. Luckily, his iPhone 7 films the scene live, and the Golani commander thinks it's a terrorist attack. He orders a jeep patrolling the sector to rush to the artificial dune. In the meantime the Bedouins work Elias over good. He manages to get away, but they catch him a hundred yards farther on and force him back to the foot of the four-wheel drive. They search him and confiscate the keys to the vehicle. One of the two then takes out a knife at the same time the army jeep surges up, saving Elias's throat from being slit. The two guys run away, but the jeep drives off after them while Elias gets up with difficulty, bruised and swollen like at the end of a ten-round fight.

Yes, he's had better moments in his life. It's as if fate's been hounding him the past few days.

He lies down with his arms stretched out on the dune and breathes in deeply to get his breath back. What luck! Incredible, even. If he'd called the Golani commander a minute later, just a minute later, he'd have been slaughtered like an animal.

The jeep comes back again with the two captured Bedouins and makes a quick stop in front of the four-wheel drive. "Hey, these must be the keys to the car. Can you come make a deposition at the end of the day?" the soldier says to him, and Elias nods as he recovers his keys.

But he feels sick over the idea of having been that lucky, and because those two guys are now in deep shit. He walks back and forth around the car, wondering if it's a good idea to call Illan, tell him the truth, and get them released. A strong feeling of guilt is beginning to rise in him. After all, he swindled those two guys, and now they're going to spend God knows how much time in the slammer. Caught red handed in an attempted assassination, you can get ten years, life for terrorism. Especially right in the middle of the knife intifada! He can't stand it. On the other hand, they would have cut his throat if the jeep hadn't gotten there on time. They wouldn't have hesitated a second.

He calls Manu to ask for advice, while Marcel is sending him text after text to send in his story on the collapse of the tunnels as soon as possible: *I programmed it for The Big Night with Danielle Godmiche, so move it!*

"On the spot like that, I don't know what to tell you," Manu confesses. "It's a bad business, seems to me. But the main thing is you're still alive."

"It's getting seriously complicated now," Diabolo mumbles. "If only you could cancel your subscription to idiocy,

Elias! But for the moment, don't budge! They tried to assassinate you with a knife, and that's it. It's a fucking terrorist attack, that's all."

"I don't want you to talk about it on *IBN*, Diabolo. Not a word!"

"What do you think I am, a fink?"

The pain of the breakup plus solitude plus moral distress! He's inside a cocktail of existential dramas with no exit, and his reporting on the collapse of the tunnels shows it. Elias is thinking only of Olga, and he keeps making slips of the tongue while recording the commentary: "Islamist olganization" for Hamas. He sends the story out at 6:00 p.m. and, in return, receives a new broadside of compliments from the ed-in-chief: "This is useless! It's pathetic! You can flush it down the toilet! I have to redo your shitty commentary!" But it hardly affects him. In any case, a lot less than the dilemma that's tormenting him. At the end of the day he drops by the Golani unit to make his deposition before going to eat in Netivot.

"The two terrorists were transferred to the Shabak," Illan tells him.

"To Shin Bet . . . the internal security service?"

"Yes, exactly. They'll decide if it's a terrorist act or a criminal act."

"OK," Elias says. "But in my opinion, it's terrorism."

"Anyway, they were caught in the act by my telephone and confirmed by the patrol," the officer concludes, handing him the deposition to sign. "Don't fall asleep in the four-wheel drive," he adds, shaking his hand. Elias takes his leave.

He snacks on a tasteless falafel in the Netivot canyon, hoping the Shabak will say it's a terrorist attack, in which case he won't have to explain himself. But that business isn't leaving him in peace for all that. His luck, if you can call it *luck*, is that they wanted to cut his throat. If they'd only tried to rip off the car, the investigation would have gone to the police, and they would have gotten to the truth in the end.

He follows the officer's advice and takes a hotel room in town, but the next day his mind is no clearer. He had confused nightmares, and he still can't find a solution to the injustice that's being perpetrated to his advantage. If he gives himself up, he's the one who'd be behind bars for embezzlement, not to mention fired for gross misconduct. In either case, he comes out the loser.

Marcel calls him at 7:00 a.m., furious: "I just got the news in a dispatch from Reuters. This is too much, Elias! You're too much!"

"OK, OK, I'm not dead."

"But the competition got the scoop, Elias! What does that make me look like?"

"It's not a scoop! There are knife attacks every day. Every day!"

"Not on a Franco-Israeli reporter! And not in the Negev!"

"Listen, Marcel, I was reluctant to call you because I'd like to be able to keep working here, and it's better not to blow up this business."

"What the hell are you saying? We have a great scoop, and you want to give it to the Yanks as a present?"

"Think, Marcel, instead of flying off the handle like an idiot! If you make me into a victim or a hero, there'll be more attacks on H24 correspondents, precisely because I'm a Franco-Israeli reporter. For the terrorists, you become an ideal target if you're making the headlines."

"In any case, you come back here. Come back immediately, Elias!" Marcel screams. "Come back to Tel Aviv right away. I don't want to have your death on my conscience!"

Which puts a full stop to his adventure as a permanent correspondent on the Gaza border. But not on his pain after the breakup, still less to his crisis of conscience about the two Bedouins. And then he didn't realize the news would spread so fast. On the way, he calls his friends in Tel Aviv.

"But they did want to cut your throat!" Manu argues, after thinking about it. "Finally, they're just getting what they deserve."

"Yeah, but shit, I swindled them! Swindled them out of twenty-five thousand bucks."

"You reimburse them, and that's it!"

"But I *spent* that bread, man! You don't get it, or what?"

"Do whatever, but I'd rather see them both in jail than you all alone six feet under," Manu adds.

When he gets back to the channel, Elias is surrounded like a hero. All the girls in the newsroom elbow their way in to kiss him, give him passionate hugs, and take historic selfies. Everything is ready for him to participate in *The Big Night*, Danielle Godmiche's show, but Elias turns down the invitation on the renewed grounds that it would expose all of them to new terrorist attacks. Everyone has different opinions about that. The pros and cons argue for a few minutes, and while he does manage to convince some of his coworkers, he has to fight every inch of the way to escape the pressure from the top. His own interest is to squelch the affair. Keep a low profile. Very, very low, in fact.

"You won't be able work in the Territories if you put what happened to me all over the media."

"But I have calls from all our Israeli colleagues to interview you," Marcel retorts.

"So refuse!"

"But we can't do that, Elias. This is hot news!"

The director of the channel and then the megadirector and then the gigadirector call him on his cell to order him to "puff it up," but Elias responds to each of them in the same way: "That's taking a considerable risk. You do think about your employees a little?" When they insist, he threatens to resign and, consequently, hush up the affair. Just a short item at the end of the news, and that's it.

Olga follows the argument from afar, and although she doesn't get into it, she does imagine the tragedy it would have been for her if he'd been assassinated just after their breakup. Surely a lasting feeling of guilt. It's only once they're all back at their computers that she goes up to Elias. "You can't imagine what I felt when I read that Reuters story. I think I would've died!"

"*Pfff* . . . it's just the risks of the profession," he answers, with a forced lone-cowboy smile as he turns away.

She grabs him by the arm and, looking him in the eyes, says, "Do take care of yourself, I don't want them to hurt you, Eli."

He walks away without looking back, praying she's beginning to kick herself for dropping him. But hardly is he outside, and he begins to cry again. It tears him apart when he sees her. A stabbing. A real one. At least on the artificial dune facing Gaza, it was out of sight, out of mind.

He'll be back in the newsroom from next Sunday on, and that will mean having Olga in his field of vision eight hours a day. Now, he spends at least six crying.

# Chapter 13

Quivering with impatience, Diabolo is driving to Ben Gurion Airport to pick up Dina Aziza. She's finally coming back after six months in South Dakota, working on her thesis. What she and Diabolo have between them, it's very Freudian. He has her father's body, overweight like him, the same ogre's laugh, and fifteen years on her. Hence the difficulty they already had in coupling before she went to live in the States for her research. But then, at that time Dina had an apartment in Tel Aviv. Now she's asked him to put her up—with her dog—for a while, before she leaves again for research in Poland. Cohabitation can only bring them closer together. *The devil take me if it doesn't end up in the same bed,* he thought.

Diabolo throws a party on the terrace that same evening in honor of Dina's return. A few dozen guests are jockeying for position around the buffet, even Romy. It's the first time she's seen Manu since that terrible evening. In the crush, they manage to avoid each other, but finally they find themselves face to face in front of the door to the bathroom. His heart starts pounding like a drum. He's incurably in love with her. But how can you love someone so much if they don't love you?

Up to now, Manu has experienced only mutual love affairs. Counting Juliette's refusal, that makes twice he's fallen flat on his face since being in Tel Aviv. Makes you wonder, doesn't it? This was never an issue when he was in porn. Married to his wife in civilian life and lover of all his partners on the job, his love life had been clear as day. No ambiguity. Divorcing and leaving the porn world modified his condition as a male. He no longer knows how you go about seducing a woman. But did he ever really know?

"I hope one day you'll . . . forgive me," he says to Romy with a choked voice and a pounding heart.

"Let's not talk about it anymore," she says, angrily. "How's the eye?"

"Dead, I think."

"I never hurt anyone, never. But what you did to me, I'll never forget it. Never!"

"One day, maybe . . ."

"No, never!"

"So in another life, maybe. Anyway, if I can help you . . ."

She locks herself in the bathroom for a few moments, and when she comes out Manu is still there, waiting for her.

"My son went back to France, you know?" she says. "So if you want his electric bike, well, come by and get it."

"Really?" asks Manu, astonished. "That's very nice of you."

"I'm giving it to you for thirty-five hundred shekels," Romy adds.

Manu doesn't dare argue about the price, although it's way too high. That's the price of a new electric bike, not a sec-ondhand one in who-knows-what condition. But as Diabolo already noticed, Romy always thinks she doesn't have any money, whereas she doesn't even have to pay rent on Dizengoff Avenue. Or else she thinks Manu is eternally in her debt, and she can tax him at will as a price for her silence. In any case, she wants 3,500 shekels for her crappy bike, and this isn't the time to pinch pennies. Manu agrees to get it tomorrow, but Romy wants cash in advance right away, now, in front of the toilets.

"All I got is three hundred."

"Give it to me," she says, without a qualm. "All of it. That way I'm sure of the sale."

She pockets everything he has on him, even two-shekel coins. She really should have made X-rated movies, Manu tells himself. She has all the greed of porn stars: their fake eyelashes flutter feverishly at the sight of the smallest banknote.

"Hey, lovers, things going well?" Dina throws out as she walks by. Even a quick glance must be enough to show that Manu is still just as mad about Romy, while she's horrible with him.

"Where the hell's that asshole Elias?" Diabolo trumpets as he walks by in his turn, with Jonathan Simsen at his heels.

"No idea," Manu answers.

"Well, call him, for godsake! It's midnight already!" And to Jonathan: "Bring up the champagne, Jojo, I'm bringing the sweets."

Now, that night, after work, Elias finally goes back to Levinsky Street to sleep—or rather he falls asleep there, after lying down for a little twilight nap. He opens his eyes only the next morning, dazzled by the first rays of the sun. It's Friday, the eve of Shabbat, his favorite day in Tel Aviv. There's a sharp drop in the city's tension and energy. From the Namal to Florentin, the bars are full of girls in high-heeled shoes, with dresses cut so low they go down to the navel whatever the weather. The appetite for life becomes almost palpable. On Fridays, people get up late and have breakfast in cafés, but as couples, families, or groups of friends. Nobody stays alone that morning of the week—except Elias, who feels like being alone. He makes a cup of coffee and goes to drink it on the terrace, still just as nauseous.

On the little balcony of his old apartment down below, he sees panties and bras drying on a line and it excites him a little, a woman now living in that tiny room. To be familiar with a neighbor's underwear before knowing what she wears can arouse uncontrollable desires in him. It makes him want to go knock on her door.

But first he goes back to pour himself a second espresso, leaf through *Zeno's Conscience*, and take a few notes for the novel he's planning. Then he goes back on the terrace. His dilemma doesn't leave him for a moment, and the pain of his breakup lingers like neuralgia. When it's not Olga, it's the two Bedouins who haunt him. One drives out the other. He's so afraid of the snowball effect of that Reuters story! Already a reporter from *Israel Hayom* got his number and left him a message to learn more about it.

Then Elias sees that the girl who replaced him in the little room below has settled in for a sunbath, stretched out on her belly. He's too high up to recognize Juliette, but he can make out that she's blonde and has a soft, curved body like Olga's. Or Juliette's, in fact. A kitten climbs up on her behind, and she brushes it away with a simple gesture of her hand. The kitten makes a backflip but lands on his mistress's butt and the game starts up again. A charming little scene that makes him think back to Jean-Pierre, of course, but above all distracts him from his two big problems.

He goes down and rings her bell under the pretext of getting his mail, and when Juliette opens the door, wearing only a little sarong, Elias shrinks back abruptly.

"Hell!" he says, stunned. "You're the one who lives here?"

She's holding the kitten in her arms to prevent him from escaping and squeezes him still more strongly when she sees Elias. Words don't come to her right away, tears do. Elias is tempted to flee, but that would be too shoddy. On the other hand, facing a woman who's crying is so disarming—a woman with whom you've behaved badly, above all, a woman you've humiliated. What's more, Juliette doesn't cry like some slut with her eye shadow melting and yelps that make you want to run away. She has her back to the wall, and she lets tears run down her cheeks in silence, like Kim Basinger in *9½ Weeks*. She's leaving the door open for him to finally come back, so she can touch him again. She missed the feel of his skin so much!

Elias finally goes in with his head down and closes the door behind him. As far as fun goes, forget it. But his old pigsty has become so stylish and cozy that it gives him a funny feeling. It even gives him some regrets. Juliette has really fixed everything up. A lamp, a jute rug, colorful cushions. Presto, it's inhabited!

He'd have to fuck her to make her stop crying, but he has absolutely no desire to fuck. As long as he didn't know it was her, he would have sex with any woman who happened to live there. Now that he knows, it's a different story. She wipes her eyes and goes to make coffee, takes out a metal cookie box like a grandma and sets it in front of him. Juliette, so beautiful, so pure, and usually so rock and roll, becomes all maternal in his presence. It exasperates Elias, but he holds himself back. Still in silence, she sets breakfast out on the low table, slices some bread, makes toast. Butter, jam, orange juice. She's not doing it on purpose, but instinctively she's acting in a way that would oblige Elias to live a normal life with her. That's it, that's exactly it, the life she wants with him: *shalom bayit*, like the religious Jews. Like Mathilde, her sister, with her husband and seven kids.

The kitten doesn't get it, of course. He frisks around, jumps, scratches Elias's jeans.

"How did you know I was living here?" she finally asks, her voice still thick with sobs.

"I didn't know. I just came by to pick up my mail," Elias answers, playing absentmindedly with Jean-Pierre.

Naturally, he wonders why this cat looks so much like the one he gave Manu. But nothing looks more like a gray cat than another gray cat, right? Impossible to imagine it's the same one. By what weird chance could she have inherited his cat? Manu isn't even supposed to know she's in Tel Aviv, Elias naively tells himself. But it becomes quite clear that it's the same cat when Juliette orders the kitty to get off the low table and calls it *Jean-Pierre*. Now that makes his skin crawl, or maybe he's having a terrible asthma attack or sinus trouble, but all those coincidences . . . it's starting to not look like coincidences. Not. At. All.

"*You* gave him that name?"

"Why do you ask?"

"Just curious."

"Well, yes," Juliette answers after a pause. Because even if she doesn't know the total truth, she can sense there's a connection between Jean-Pierre and Elias, and it goes through Manu.

"Y'know, it's totally weird, you with a kitten called Jean-Pierre when I gave Manu a kitten whose name was Jean-Pierre too. And they resemble each other like two peas in a pod."

The last thing Juliette wants is for him to use this pretext to leave her again in a burst of anger, so she takes still more time to answer as she butters his toast.

"Can you explain that?" he insists.

"First explain why you humiliated me," she finally says.

"I didn't humiliate you!" Elias protests. "I was living my own life, and you showed up at the wrong time, that's all."

"But you knew I was coming."

"No, you were supposed to come the day before. I thought you'd changed your mind, and besides, I didn't ask you to come live with me."

She gives him the piece of toast and watches him chew, still as hungry, still that voracious appetite, and Juliette, practically naked under her short bathrobe with her nipples pressing up against the silk, overcome with love for this ogre, feels herself irremediably slipping into his arms when she shouldn't do that. Her head leans toward him as if despite herself, rests on his chest, and she sinks into a state that's worse than abandonment and resignation—a state of surrender, that's the word. She cannot resist her attraction to this guy, and she gets carried away with no restraint whatsoever, hugging him, kissing him, caressing him; all the dams of distrust collapse one after the other. That's what passion does. After a first breakup, you feel even more like having sex together. Argument revives eroticism; a breakup arouses desire; reunions are torrid, and as soon as you touch each other again, you have a lot less need for explanations. They missed the other's skin too much, and the tough questions are put on hold indefinitely. Elias will never know how she inherited a cat, and she'll never know what he had boiling in his pot to humiliate her like that when she arrived in Tel Aviv. In any case, they won't talk about it again that morning.

One day he told her: "Together, I don't have any strength." And yet, all the tension that had accumulated since Olga left him and all his paranoia after the two Bedouins attacked him was calmed down when he made love again with Juliette. He owes her that, at least, and if that's not literally strength, it's still a great benefit. But what next? Is it even possible to go out in the street with her? Conceivable? Olga would know about it in real time, you can bet on it! And the faint hope he has of getting her back some day would definitively disappear. Rumors spread so fast among the French in Tel Aviv. A new can of worms for Elias. A new torment. Every one of his acts drags him into a new mess, or another source of embarrassment or paranoia. He's caught in a spiral he can't manage to break. A fate worse than a fatwa.

Hardly has he calmed down than he's tormented again. Angry once again. He gets dressed.

"Stay awhile, please," Juliette begs.

Marco Koskas

"Manu's the one who gave you that cat?"

"Don't screw me like a whore. Please, Elias . . . I love you."

"Answer me, I need to know."

"No, I found it in the street."

"OK, I'll come by again tonight," he says.

"Promise?"

"No, but I'll come by."

"What time will you come by, Manu?" Romy asks him.

"I can't this afternoon," Manu answers.

"So when?" she asks in an imperious tone.

"I'll call you in a while to tell you. I've got a client coming in around five."

"OK, I'll wait for your call till Shabbat, and that's it," she warns. Manu realizes right away she's not going to give up just because of the day of rest. It's a deadline she's given him, an ultimatum. Beyond that time, God knows what she could do. What chutzpah! He'd ruin himself for her, not for her shitty bike.

At that moment the doorbell rings, and Manu opens it.

"Hey, Elias. Come in. Want a cup of coffee?"

"No, I'm good. I'm just coming to get Jean-Pierre."

Manu tries again to spin him a yarn about the cat, but Elias interrupts brusquely. "Stop lying," he tells him in an icy tone. "You gave my cat to Juliette, and I want to know why."

There follows a violent argument between the two friends, with Manu claiming Juliette was so distraught by Elias's betrayal that he didn't have the heart to refuse to give her the cat.

"Imagine me giving something you gave me to your ex, Manu! Just think! You'd like that? You're a total asshole!"

"Calm down, Elias. You did make me take that cat."

"All you had to do was say no!"

"Oh, sure, I should've—"

"And she sucked you off, I know it, she told me!"

"Bullshit!"

"You could be her father, for godsake! You're not ashamed?"

"Are you off your rocker, Elias?"

"You're disgusting, Manu! As if there weren't enough chicks in Tel Aviv, you gotta fuck my exes! At your age, for shit's sake, at your age!"

"So why does that bother you, since it's your ex?"

"It bothers me because you did it behind my back! I don't trust you anymore!"

"No, it bothers you because you went and fucked her again!"

"That's not true!"

Elias leaves, slamming the door behind him. It was too good a friendship—too good to last. At the same time, Manu is sure it will blow over, because Elias's reaction comes from pride and panic.

But Manu also sees the connection between this clash with Elias and his two last failures with women. Maybe it's connected to his age, but not only. Since he left pornography, he's been trying to reconstruct the family he wants, and it's not working. The foundation is probably bad. He's building on sand. His status as a sexagenarian makes him out of place in all situations where there might be a sexual relationship. For porn actors are a family. He wanted to cast off his moorings and live like a young man, and now he's drifting around without a rudder. His unhappiness suddenly becomes blindingly clear to him. He hasn't slept with a woman for a year, and the last one he slept with was an ex–movie partner.

Slightly before 5:45 p.m., the beginning of Shabbat, Romy returns to the attack.

"My renters haven't come yet," he claims, to justify himself.

"I don't give a damn! I want my bread!" she shouts. "Listen, Manu: either you come get the bike in the next hour, or I press charges against you for attempted rape. Got it? Attempted rape!"

# CHAPTER 14

Juliette cancels her Shabbat at Mathilde's in Pisgat Ze'ev to stay with Elias, while Diabolo has a date on Shabazi Street with a certain Amande (or Amandine or Amanda, he's not sure), with whom something will surely happen, even if it is a job interview. No woman can resist Diabolo, despite his 310 pounds of fat. Aside from Dina, who is resisting . . .

Around five o'clock, Juliette comes back from the beach where she spent the afternoon with Jonathan, Diabolo's assistant. He's always after her, and she finds him quite nice, but she leaves him no hope. While she waits for Elias to come back to her place, Juliette tries on all her clothes, puts on a little perfume, and retouches her makeup, smiling again and brimming with life. The passionate morning she spent with Elias and then the afternoon on Banana Beach have given her fair skin a golden aura, and when Juliette is radiant like that, no woman is as beautiful as she is. But where does he even live?

She forgot to ask him! So strongly was she attached to his skin, to his smell. Has there ever been someone as mad about a guy as she is about Elias? Sometimes it makes her laugh. But not often. Most of the time it scares her. If only he would send her a little text from time to time to temper the mixture of desire and anxiety she's feeling. Or to feed into it. Or to show he's in the same mood. But nothing. Not a word. Never the heavenly surprise of seeing his name pop up on the screen of her old Sony. You'd think smartphones were invented for nothing. As for her, she doesn't dare send him little loving messages, either, as girls do with their guy. She's too afraid of exasperating him. And no naked selfies. It's not because she doesn't want to, you know . . . Manu took supersuggestive photos on the balcony and the couch when she lived with him—her hair undone, her legs gaping, her skirt raised—and it had excited her a little. Actually, she does like to show off. Too bad she doesn't dare. Where does that shyness come from, actually? That unpleasant feeling of having to walk on eggs all the time? Of being just barely tolerated, despite all the guys running after her? What did she do wrong to pay such a price?

Around eight, she has the feeling he's not going to come, and at nine she admits it's all over. And of course, he's impossible to contact. At ten she goes out and starts wandering around the Tayelet. On Friday nights, there isn't a soul in the streets before eleven. People have dinner with their families and go out afterward. Juliette walks by only Arabs from Yafo drumming on their cars to bug everybody and because it's the only time of the week when they can think the seaside belongs to them. She dreams of a gigantic, implacable tsunami—a tsunami that would carry her off. Let's get it over with! Her phone chimes, but it's never Elias, just the ritual *shabbat shalom* from her pals in Jeru. Not even sorry. Bastard. Son of a bitch. What cruelty! She got ready for him, with an off-the-shoulder satin top and her hair styled so he would want to be with her, and instead of that he stands her up. He can go fuck himself!

She walks up toward Rothschild because among the rare bars open on Friday night, there's the Cofix on Lilienblum Street. When people are broke and want to get smashed cheap, that's where they go. Everything's five shekels. Whiskey, Coke, vodka, or beer, same price. It's full of Russians, already drunk and haggard, blue eyes with red whites, three hairs on their chins, black fingernails, still knocking it back again and again just to roll under the table grunting, and young Frenchmen without a cent, bombed for only thirty shekels. Elias might be hanging out there. But she narrowly misses him. She bumps into Yoni, her Jeru pal who eats pork with a yarmulke on his head. He informs her that Elias just left not five minutes earlier. Actually, Olga told him on the phone, "I have to talk to you, it's urgent." That's why he left. But Yoni doesn't know that. He just saw Elias jump up and disappear as if he'd been sucked out of Cofix.

Juliette goes off again, leaving behind her a wake of bitter tears and crumbs of her broken heart. At the corner of Herzl, she bumps into Manu, who resigned himself to walking over to Romy's to pick up the bike even though it's close to midnight, and on a Friday night there are no buses and very few taxis. At any rate, he'd needed to go by the ATM of the Bank Leumi at the corner of Yehuda Halevi Street and then maybe try to get a *sherut* on the corner of Allenby and Rothschild—he could ask the shared taxi to take him to Dizengoff—but in short, he didn't get there either, and what's more he could only take out two thousand shekels. Despite the advance he'd already given her, it's not enough. So he's afraid of Romy's reaction.

"You wouldn't have a thousand shekels to lend me till Sunday?" he asks Juliette feverishly. "Well, twelve hundred."

"Not on me, no," Juliette answers in a trembling voice and immediately snuggles into Manu's arms. "He betrayed me again, that bastard!" she sobs. "I can't take it anymore, Manu! I can't take it!"

Always present at the most heartbreaking times of her melodrama, Manu seems to have become Juliette's official guardian angel, her prophet Elijah. The fact that she had sucked him once changed nothing in their relationship. He will never be her lover. Her protector, yes: the most solid, safest shoulder in all Tel Aviv. That's it. Manu hugs her affectionately, but even without thinking about sex, he gets a hard-on. It probably comes from his old job, an unconscious conditioned

reflex, for he's still extremely anxious about Romy. On tenter-
hooks, in fact. Not at all in the mood for sex. He is so afraid
she'll press charges!

"How much a week can you take out?" he asks Juliette, for
this time his own anxiety prevails over her situation.

"Can you imagine? This morning he came to my place by
mistake and just screwed me! That bastard! I'd die for him! Just
to screw me!"

"Yeah, I know," Manu says. "He came by my place afterward. We got into a real fight, if you want to know."

Together, they go to the ATM of the Bank Leumi, and
Juliette withdraws five hundred shekels for him. That's all her
weekly limit will allow. Not one cent more. At least that will
make two thousand eight hundred in all, and when you take
into account the advance he paid, not that far from the full
amount.

"You won't be mad if I cut out now?"

"But why're you leaving? Stay with me, Manu. Please,"
Juliette begs.

"Well then, walk with me. I'm going to try and grab a
*sherut* for Dizengoff."

She takes his arm, and they walk up the central thorough-
fare together to Japanika Sushi at the intersection of Rothschild
and Allenby, like a couple out together on Shabbat eve after the
family dinner, melting into the crowd already gathering there.

"You might've told me Jean-Pierre was his cat," Juliette remarks as they cross.

"I got a call from Amos Kirzenbaum, you know, darling."

"Who's he?" Elias asks.

"The blogger on *Tag Shalom*," Olga answers.

"What about?"

"The terrorist attack on you."

Olga is on duty this Friday night at H24, and it makes a funny impression on Elias to see her in private conversation in the deserted newsroom. They look like two survivors of a shipwreck, for when this open-space office isn't buzzing like a hive, it makes you think of an ocean liner that's been hastily evacuated, with its computers off, its chairs empty, and its whitish lights. But did Olga call him just about this, or because she's starting to miss him? They've hardly started talking, and already there are stealthy glances and restrained gestures between them.

"You sure his name is Amos Kirzenbaum?" Elias asks.

"Well, yeah, why?"

"Because Amos Kirzenbaum is the name of the main character of my novel, and he's also a member of a pro-Palestinian NGO."

"That gives me the shivers," she whispers, rubbing her arm vigorously.

"What did he want from you?" Elias asks, in a low, worried voice.

"Nothing from me. You're the one he wanted to talk to," she answers, crossing her legs just under his nose. "That is, he was trying to reach you, and they passed him to me."

"Did you give him my number?"

"No, I thought I'd better ask you first," Olga says, leaning toward him.

"And so?"

She puts her two hands on his thigh, as if they could take liberties with each other again, and looking him in the eye, she says: "Eli darling . . . tell me what happened with the two Bedouins. I'm on your side, you know. I love you. Trust me."

Naturally, he can't believe his ears, so much has he dreamed of this moment and so much did he not believe it would happen. Besides, what should he answer? The question about the Bedouins or that "I love you" dropped from the sky? All in the same sentence! And with that languorous look like on the first day. As if she'd never given him that cruel moment when she got back from Gérardmer, as if the return of affections promised by all the witch doctors in the world existed in reality.

"You love me?" he repeats incredulously. "What're you talking about, I mean, I thought you didn't, I thought it was over. What do you mean you love me?"

"Yes, I love you and I miss you. I made a mistake and—"

"A mistake!" Elias interrupts her with a shout. "You kidding me? Or . . ."

"I'm young, that's all, that's why," she says defensively. "Young and stupid, so forgive me."

"But I almost died, for godsake! Died for you, almost killed myself. Ask Manu. I lost twenty pounds, shit, touch me, I'm just a skeleton because you made a mistake."

"Forgive me, darling, I didn't realize . . . but if you still want me, we . . . well, the hell with it, we'll start over."

"The hell . . ."

Without waiting for the rest of his sentence, she straddles Elias, and in that movement her skirt goes up to the top of her thighs. She wraps her arms around him and squeezes herself against him with her mouth plunged into his for a syrupy soup of tongues. Aside from the surveillance cameras, no one's watching them, for the simple reason that no one's there, and if it weren't for the business with the two Bedouins still sticking around in his conscience, it would have been the best day in Elias's life.

There remains the disconcerting and troubling coincidence between Amos Kirzenbaum, whom he'd imagined as the last Jew in Tel Aviv after the disappearance of the State of Israel, and the pro-Palestinian blogger who tried to reach him. Disconcerting and troubling not only because of their common name, but also because of what characterizes the Amos Kirzenbaum he had imagined. For that Amos is a traitor—a storybook traitor, paid by the enemies of Israel, a traitor without knowing it but still a traitor, paid by immensely wealthy

Qataris. But the Amos Kirzenbaum who tried to reach him, is he the same type of guy?

Olga and Elias leave the offices of H24 and walk to her place on Derech Yerushalaim for a sleepless night of reunion. He holds her firmly by the arm, and that's solid, not a hollow dream. And yet he still doesn't believe in the reality of this miraculous return of the beloved. He tells himself she's just acting on a whim that must have caught her by surprise because she was bored stiff sitting by herself in the newsroom, and tomorrow she'll leave him again. So he doesn't get carried away either. Or rather, yes, he gets carried away sexually, but his heart remains on the lookout. He doesn't answer the little loving words Olga whispers to him in bed—not because he doesn't want to whisper some others too. His mouth is full of such words. Besides, they're more like shouts than words, a strange mix of coarse language and sobs he does well to swallow back.

Before she falls asleep, Olga returns to the question that brought them together again: "Eli dearest, answer me this time: What exactly happened with the two Bedouins?"

"Well, they tried to stab me, and it was filmed by my iPhone."

"Tell me why, my love," she stammers, closing her eyes, and she falls asleep without getting an answer.

Elias lies there with his eyes open, wondering what sixth sense this girl has to suspect he's not telling her everything.

Can he tell her that in essence it's pretty much because of her that everything happened? Well, not exactly because of her, but because of the jewel he wanted to give her, because of the ambition of a starry-eyed lover and that desire to give more than you have to the woman you love. And blondes are supposed to be dumb! This one has the sharpest mind he's ever known.

But he can't manage to fall asleep and clicks through the Israeli information sites to see if they might possibly be talking about his affair. Now, that very evening, jihadists slaughtered people at the Bataclan, the Stade de France, and on sidewalk cafés. Paris is running with blood. At least 130 dead. The whole world's attention is focused on France. His little affair isn't mentioned anywhere, except for a brief item on *Haaretz*. He's annoyed with himself for feeling relieved, naturally. But he's relieved all the same. The tragedy in Paris has made him fall into oblivion, like an ill wind that blows somebody good. At the same time, he prays to heaven that Dani, his little brother who loves heavy metal so much, isn't in the group of victims at the Bataclan and his father wasn't in the Stade de France that night to see the French soccer team. And that none of his buddies had the bad idea of sitting down at the Carillon Café.

# Chapter 15

"Are you presenting yourself with your second?" Romy asks mockingly, seeing Manu has come with someone.

"No, no, she's just a friend. Juliette, this is Romy." Romy grants Juliette a vague nod and takes the stack of bills. She counts them, wetting her finger.

"There's still a little missing," Manu admits. "But I'll make up the whole thing by Sunday. I couldn't withdraw more from the ATM."

"Sunday, final deadline for liquidating this business," she warns as she pockets the money. Then she walks them to the door and locks it behind them twice without even saying goodbye.

"How about that?" Juliette says, once they're outside. "She sure is tough, your ladylove!"

"She has a hard life, that's why. It's no fun cleaning apartments."

"Huh! She really cleans apartments?" Juliette asks, taking Manu's arm.

"Yes, this is her father's apartment. She doesn't pay rent, but she has to struggle to make a few shekels."

"I understand."

Instead of going through the Tayelet to go back to Florentin, they turn on Ben Gurion Street and walk up Ben Yehuda, while watching to see if there could be a *sherut* behind them. But when they get to the intersection of Frishman and Ben Yehuda, they see that Café Mersand is open that evening, whereas it's always closed on the eve of Shabbat, so they cross the street and sit down. Juliette can hold her drink, but she still needs three glasses of Chardonnay before she dares ask Manu the question that's obsessing her.

"Tell me where he lives exactly, please, Manu."

"Who?"

"You know very well."

"Across from your place, in the high-rise," Manu answers, after some hesitation.

All sorts of situations that this proximity can create go through her head, but she doesn't connect Elias's sudden appearance that very morning to what Manu has just revealed to her. She still thinks it was a coincidence that Elias came by to pick up his mail. The worst would be to bump into him coming and going with one of his girls. The best would be to see him, if only to glimpse him, even a fleeting glimpse, but alone, taking out the trash or going shopping at AM:PM or Shuk Levinsky, who cares as long as he's alone. She'd be so happy! Then she'd go demand an explanation from him, even though she does feel she's not very important to him. She also admits she was wrong to want to impose her presence on him in Tel Aviv. He's a pretty unsociable man, guards his freedom jealously. A kind of artist. Or a fanatical individualist. Certainly not a husband and still less the possible father of her future children. And then there's the fact that he never did his military service, as she did. He's not a true Israeli.

He doesn't know what it's like to risk your life at eighteen, go to sleep all muddy and exhausted after a twenty-mile march with a pack on your back, be one of nine conscripts in a tiny tent, share the little food you have, or lower your voice so a comrade in the unit can talk to her parents on the phone. They may drink the milk of the same mother tongue, but they weren't raised in the same culture. Trying to contain the sorrow that's devastating her, that's Juliette's reasoning. But the pain of love is always stronger, alas. It resists reason and analysis. Reason helps a little, but it's just a crutch, not a cure.

The third big affair of her life and the third washout. Another man who doesn't want her, while so many others grovel at her feet.

"I'm just cursed," she sighs out of the blue and without even having followed her train of thought.

"Come on, stop the bullshit!" Manu says.

A funny Shabbat, no breaking bread or blessing wine, just drinking a glass of dry white in the melancholy of this windy night in Tel Aviv while Paris counts its dead. On Facebook,

French tricolor flags are beginning to cover the outline of all the photos, and the slogan of solidarity—"I am Paris"—is proliferating on the social networks. But Juliette's head is elsewhere. She doesn't even know about the Paris massacres. As soon as she gets up the next day, she begins watching the people entering and leaving Elias's building. For three hours, her staring eyes don't leave the door that opens and shuts regularly, releasing its batches of the faithful with tallits on their shoulders, its yuppies with round Ray-Bans, its tattooed girls and guys in flip-flops despite the cold, families of Tel Avivian bourgeois bohemians with their dear blonde heads and their dogs. There are so many people in a high-rise like that.

Sitting on her little balcony, Juliette doesn't miss a trick, but she feels herself turning into a surveillance camera, not even daring to go pee for fear of missing Elias. Her patience is finally rewarded in the middle of the afternoon, when he arrives at last, with Olga. So she's the one, the girl he's crazy about! Another blonde, but taller and more languid. A rich man's daughter, you can see it in her walk. Yet they had separated, according to Manu. So they got together again! Or it's someone else. Juliette feels like shouting his name, just to make him flip out. But nothing comes out of her throat. No, decidedly, she's not ready yet to see him going by without breaking her heart. What's more, going by with another girl!

# CHAPTER 16

The next day is Sunday, the first business day of the week, and the press is talking only about the Paris attacks. From *Israel Hayom* to *Haaretz*, almost every page is devoted to that. The Promised Land has tears in its eyes, and Tel Aviv is dumbfounded. Despite the unkind way the French often view their own country, Israelis have a weakness for France, that unfaithful friend. And they tremble for her, as if they knew she is too fragile or too innocent to survive such ordeals. After the *Charlie Hebdo* massacre, the Bataclan. An editorialist in *Yedioth Ahronoth* even wonders how their friend France is going to get out of this situation if it doesn't get rid of its colonial guilt toward Arabs.

That morning, before going to H24, Elias and Olga create a group on WhatsApp to make their relationship official. At least that way there's no more need to curb their gestures or sneak around, and they spend a great part of the morning thanking coworkers who come over and congratulate them. The Shabbat holiday allowed people to get back to a normal state of mind after the previous day's attacks. Even if they're still talking about it a lot that morning, one hit drives out the other, and the news of the day is the officialization of the Olga-Elias couple. Danielle Godmiche hugs them both in her arms, already proposing to be a witness at their wedding. She even declares, "You're really made for one another, I knew it, it's just incredible!"

They all go ahead with their little compliments, their good wishes and even blessings, despite the little pangs and inevitable regrets of the men and women who easily could have seen themselves in Olga's place or Elias's. In order for this new situation not to get in the way of the proper functioning of the newsroom, Marcel installs the two lovers at two ends of the room. And then to work! The Paris attacks become the burning topic of the day again.

Just before lunch, Elias gets a call from Illan, the Golani officer in Nahal Oz, telling him that the Shabak interrogated the two Bedouins at length and concluded it was not a terrorist attack. So the affair is going to be redefined as a criminal affair, and the two guys will be handed over to the police.

"What does that change for me?" Elias asks, worried.

"Well, it's another judicial procedure, and you'll be questioned too. So that's what changes. I just wanted to warn you."

From her workstation at the other end of the newsroom, Olga sees Elias going pale and vaguely guesses he must have heard something serious; she hopes it's not bad news from Paris. She walks over to check, but when he senses her approaching, Elias manages a spectacular change of mood in a fraction of a second, an inner revolution at the speed of light, and raises his head with a marvelous, loving smile on his lips. Olga immediately gives up questioning him. She'd tried again last night to learn what really happened with the two Bedouins on the dune, and after a while he got impatient. No point going there. If he's smiling, everything must be OK.

Still, in her heart, she's convinced he hasn't told her the whole truth. What can she do to make him trust her completely? She'd so like to be at his side whatever adversity he might face, united like fingers on a hand. But he has an insatiable desire for freedom, and she knows that will limit their mad love.

At the end of the day, Elias meets Manu at Florentin 10, and they make up.

"We'll forget everything, OK?" Elias suggests.

"OK, we'll forget everything."

"But I still can't fucking believe you took her in for two weeks without telling me."

"Yeah, well, I really felt sorry for her."

"Just imagine I take in your ex on the sly!" Elias yells, ready to start all over again.

Diabolo comes in time to stop the argument from resuming, and they order a bottle of Merlot.

"I have some good news and some bad news," Elias then announces.

"First the good news," Diabolo says.

"I got together with Olga again, and we're . . . well, we'll definitely get married."

"Mazel tov!" says Manu.

"Nice!" says Diabolo.

"But I'm getting ahead of myself a little. In reality, I don't know. We'll see . . . I'm not ready."

"And the bad news?" Diabolo asks.

"The Shabak says it's not a terrorist attack, that business. So they gave the case to the cops."

"You need a lawyer, I'm calling Jérémie Azencot," Diabolo says.

He walks off to make the call, while Yoni comes to sit down at the next table with his yarmulke on his head and his PowerBook under his arm. Elias introduces him to Manu and pours him a glass of Merlot, but Yoni doesn't engage in conversation. He just tells Elias he bumped into Juliette two nights ago at Cofix, and she was looking for him like a madwoman. Elias says, "Yes, yes," with irritation, and Yoni concentrates on his screen. Leaning discreetly over the screen, Manu sees Yoni opened a page called "A Euro for the Gaza Zoo," and he raises his eyebrows.

"You working for the S.P.A. or what?" he asks him jovially.

"No, I need money," Yoni retorts.

"What is it?" Elias says.

"A fund-raiser for marmosets," Yoni says, showing him the page he designed.

They crack up. On the internet, nothing looks more like a charity than a big swindle. But this one has definite comic potential in the way it makes a mockery of the naive optimism of charitable souls.

"You'll earn big with that," Manu predicts.

"I just need seven hundred bucks," Yoni says.

Then Diabolo comes back with a message from his lawyer to Elias. "It's not sure you'll be summoned, but if they do, Jérémie will go with you. You can call him tomorrow."

Dina Aziza joins them next with her dog, always inseparable, then in comes Maia, Yoni's girlfriend, then Danielle Godmiche, and the circle keeps growing.

"This is Manu—you know, the friend I told you about," Elias says to Danielle.

"Oh yes, Manu Goffredo!" she says. "I so admire porn stars . . ."

"This a joke, or what?" Manu grumbles, scowling.

"Not at all!" Danielle protests. "I think they're incredibly detached."

Then Juliette walks by, and the conversations on the Flo 10 terrace suddenly become evasive, as they wait to see if she's going to join them. Juliette hesitates a moment, but finally comes over and boldly sits down facing Elias but slightly at a slant, next to Maia. They knew each other in Jerusalem and immediately start chatting away as if nothing had happened. Manu's not sure if he should give Juliette a kiss as he normally would or preserve his recent reconciliation with Elias by ignoring her, while Diabolo, who only knows Juliette from her photo, plunges his nose into his email. Muttered conversations between two silences, nothing else. Embarrassment reigns. Only Danielle, unaware of the situation, wonders why the hell they all suddenly lowered their voices. Could this blonde be a star, to intimidate everyone so much?

"I so like what you do," she says to Juliette with a big smile, on the off chance she's right. Juliette looks at her wide eyed in bewilderment.

As for Elias, he feels like smashing the bottle of Merlot. He only holds himself back by staring at the heater glowing over their table. Is she ever going to let go of him? Or go to the devil? Or just go fuck herself? He had his reasons for not going back to see her Friday night, and those reasons were way more pressing than the pain he caused her. Should he have given up the love of his life for an affair of no importance? And besides, taking his apartment on Levinsky Street—what was that plan, if not harassment? Always that same gluey way of glomming on to him and following him like his shadow!

After two or three minutes of inner boiling, he suddenly gets up and goes off without even saying goodbye.

"I'll send you Azencot's number," Diabolo calls out to him.

Once he's gone, the table lightens up. Juliette asks Manu if he went to get the bike at Romy's.

"What bike?" Diabolo says, laughing up his sleeve.

"Uh . . . Romy's son's bike," Manu confesses, shamefaced.

"She gave you his bike?" Diabolo asks mockingly.

"By the way, you two don't know each other yet," says Manu, introducing Juliette to him to change the conversation.

"Thanks to you, Juliette, *IBN* got a hundred thousand visitors the same day," Diabolo tells her.

"Well, I'm happy for you," Juliette answers pleasantly. "But I wish the terrorist had picked someone else."

"So, Manu, to return to the subject, she gave you the bike?" Diabolo asks, poker faced.

"Not at all, why would she give it to me?"

"You bought if from her for how much?"

"Two thousand. Well, twenty-five hundred."

"Not thirty-five hundred?" Juliette says, putting her foot in it.

"Ha ha ha!" Diabolo guffaws. "Thirty-five hundred bucks for that old piece of crap. Man, she's greedy, that Romy!"

"Hey, here are your five hundred bucks," Manu answers in an irritated voice, giving Juliette five one-hundred-shekel bills.

As she goes back to Levinsky Street, Juliette wonders how much time went by between the moment she got to Florentin 10 and the moment Elias left. A quarter of an hour? An hour? It was such an intense moment she really thought she'd faint. But she lost the notion of time, since Elias didn't remain more than three minutes in her presence. She just remembers that she didn't understand whatever Yoni's fiancée, Maia, was telling her, and her heart was drumming in her chest so loudly she had the impression everyone could hear it. Now she feels rather proud of facing that situation and not retreating. Would she be able to do it again? Now she has no more energy, as if she lost all her strength in that face-to-face with Elias. She'd just like to go to sleep. But her mother is waiting for her at the door.

"Oh, Mom, forgive me, I'm totally zapped."

"That's nice."

"No, it's because you know, because of . . . I was kept back at the gallery by, um, you know, well, the inventory."

"Don't worry, darling, I just got here."

Juliette opens the door, and her mother discovers the little studio she now lives in on Levinsky Street in Tel Aviv.

"Well, it's very cute!"

"You think so?"

"Except you had a better apartment in Jeru."

"I've got a little balcony, you see it? Jean-Pierre!" Juliette cries, and the kitty pops out of who knows where. She takes him in her arms and presents him to Sandrine, who can't get over it.

"So Jean-Pierre is a cat?"

"It can't be a man, since no man wants me."

"What are you talking about, darling?"

"I'm dead, Mom, d'you mind if I go to bed?"

"Without eating dinner?"

"I don't feel like it."

"Go to bed, dear. I'll read."

Sandrine settles into the window seat, while Juliette goes to bed fully dressed without taking off her makeup or brushing her teeth. Her mother spares her a comment and dives into the memoirs of Father de Foucauld, a priest, but also a womanizer, at least before he went into the Church, a little like Victor. But there's no use, Juliette is turning this way and that, unable to sleep. She finally turns on her bed lamp.

"You're not sleeping?"

"Well, no, I'm too tired," she answers as she gets up. She goes and takes off her makeup and brushes her teeth. Then she gets undressed and puts on pajamas.

"What're you reading, Mom?" she asks distractedly as she goes back to bed.

"The memoirs of Father de Foucauld."

"Another priest!" Juliette sighs.

"It's very interesting, you know."

"OK, good night, Mom."

"Good night, darling."

Juliette puts out the light and turns toward the wall, while Sandrine points her pen lamp on the book and starts reading again. But she senses Juliette isn't really sleeping, and that prevents her from concentrating. Why isn't she sleeping, her darling daughter? What is bothering her so much? Sometimes she would so like to be a little mouse. See everything that's happening in her life and understand what's making her suffer so much. Not a minute goes by that she doesn't think of Juliette. If only she could take the weight of that absurd filiation off her shoulders! Because at bottom, she knows very well what's making her daughter suffer so much. *A priest's daughter, God forgive me.* And yet Moshe, her ex-husband, hadn't treated any of the three kids differently! He gave as much to Juliette as to Mathilde and Assaf. Not an iota of preference. What a great man! Yet there was no lack of gossip throughout her pregnancy. Well-meaning souls told tales, even writing poison pen letters. Good old Moshe, he would throw all those papers into the wastebasket! And never the slightest allusion to a poison pen letter. Not like Victor. Maybe he was a great man, too, but not always charitable! When Juliette was five, Sandrine wanted the priest at least to see the adorable child he had given her. But he turned away. Another time, they met by chance on a bus in Jerusalem, and he slunk off.

To be the daughter of a man who does not wish to be your father, who does not even want to know what you look like, what a nasty gift of life! Oh, how she would like to have the courage to tell her the truth. Who knows if it would help her? Such a beautiful girl, who only falls for selfish men exactly like Victor. It really makes you think, doesn't it? Is it fate? But every time she's going to do it, Sandrine shrinks back. At the last minute, she tells herself, *What's the good?* She just doesn't have the courage to confess the truth to Juliette. Yet the ideal opportunity has come, and she owes it to herself to take advantage of it: Victor Boussagol passed away three days ago at the age of eighty-one. Isn't it time to own up? To break that long silence? It's the very reason Sandrine came to Tel Aviv. Announce to Juliette that her dad is dead. Well, no way—she can't manage to do it. Petrified in her guilt. Dead or alive, Victor still decides what she has a right to say and what she must keep silent.

Too bad she doesn't know that ever since Juliette was a little girl, she'd heard that truth a thousand times. At school or in Sandrine's family, there was no dearth of allusions to it. She knew who Victor Boussagol was and what he looked like. Sandrine is torturing herself for nothing. Or she's torturing herself too late.

# CHAPTER 17

Elias answers the police summons without a lawyer to try to play down the situation, and he goes there by bus. Two hours on the road separate Tel Aviv from Netivot, that little town in the Negev a little over three miles from Gaza, and even if it isn't at the end of the world, when you want to go there, it takes all day. Despite the quantities of missiles it received from Hamas, Netivot has remained a place both calm and strange, where you sometimes meet transsexuals who've had very successful surgery. There Elias knows a certain Levana, a good-looking blonde with the voice of an ogre, very nice and ultrafeminine, who doesn't always make you pay for a blow job. A real subject for an Israeli film, that Levana: born in a man's body, but also into an ultraorthodox family who called it the work of the devil when she decided to change sex. Levana became a woman nonetheless. Her seven brothers accepted it, since she supports them financially while they twiddle their thumbs pretending to study the Torah.

As he doesn't want his absence to make waves at H24, Elias calls in sick, except that he's obliged to admit to Olga that he's going to the cops in Netivot. She frowns, quick to sense something wrong.

"Why the cops?" she asks first. "It's a terrorist attack, not a crime."

"The Shabak reclassified the attack as a criminal case."

"Why didn't you tell me?"

"Oh, no reason, just didn't want to worry you."

"Eli darling, trust me, please," she says, putting her arms around him. "Tell me what really happened. You can't leave me out of this. I'm your woman."

"Don't forget, they wanted to slit my throat."

"But you say yourself the Shabak doesn't think it's a terrorist attack."

"So what?" Elias replies. "It's still attempted murder, right?"

"Yes, but why? Why did these guys want to kill you?"

"To steal the car, that's all. Why complicate things?"

Another source of unease is growing between them— the bracelet he wanted to give her when she returned from Gérardmer. Olga doesn't dare ask for it, of course. She's too sensitive for that. But still . . .

Why doesn't he give it to her again? Well, so as not to admit it's precisely because of that damn piece of jewelry that it all happened. Elias is more or less convinced it brought him bad luck. Ill-gotten gain, an unlucky object, a jinx, whatever, he has to give it away, sell it back, or fence it, anything except give it to Olga again. He loves her so much! If she left him again, this time he'd really commit suicide.

"Do you know the two individuals who tried to assassinate you?" the Netivot policeman asks him directly.

"Never saw 'em before," Elias answers.

"They're saying they know you."

"From where?"

"They say you sold them a car and you returned to take it back in the middle of the night."

"What car?"

"The four-wheel drive you had when you got to the artificial dune."

"Baloney. That car is still at H24."

"You're not getting what I'm asking: Did you sell them the car and then take it back?"

"I never sold a car to anyone."

"That's not exactly what I'm asking. Listen up. This is my question: Did you sell them that car? Answer that already."

"Well, no."

"So you couldn't take it back from them?"

"That's logical."

"OK, so I'll let you go. But I'm going to have to check your schedule. Where were you the night of the theft?"

"When was that?" Elias asks, seeing the trap.

"The night of November fourth to the fifth."

Elias looks at his calendar in his phone. "At home."

"You have witnesses?"

"No. On the fourth, I got back to Tel Aviv around eight, and I went to the station the next day because the car had a problem."

"What problem?"

"I don't know anything about cars, but the engine kept misfiring, so I brought it back to the station garage."

"OK, would you sign here, thanks, *yalla,* you can go."

It was only five minutes of questioning, and yet Elias leaves exhausted, sure the truth will soon come out. Explode, even. Not that the cops can confound him, but his guilty conscience has reached its limit. When he gets to the bus stop, he turns around and heads back toward the police station to confess everything. Suddenly he can't stand the torment, all this shit. Sick of this business! Resigned to spend three or four months in preventive detention, he just hopes with a good lawyer he'll quickly be released on parole. Then there will be a trial and then who knows? Probably a suspended sentence since he's never been convicted of anything before, and the two Bedouins did try to cut his throat, after all. Of course he'll also lose his job. Not tragic either. But Olga? How will she take it? Will she support him? Will they remain lovers? Elias has a secret admiration for the wives of bad guys: the most faithful imaginable, the most in love, in fact. But Olga is so young. So bourgeois, too. Not a bad-guy's wife for anything in the world. At least, that's what he imagines.

At the idea of losing her a second time, he gets nauseous and throws up his whole breakfast at the foot of a tree. A few passersby stop and ask if he needs help, but he shakes his head and stands, telling himself, "Shit, I'm not gonna go into the slammer and lose Olga again! Sleep outside, own nothing, no problem. Jail, no! Never!" Anything but prison. He'd rather have a guilty conscience 24-7. So he goes off again in the opposite direction and barely catches the bus back to Tel Aviv. If the truth is really going to come out, then let it! But he's not going to help.

When he's back in town, he walks to Kerem without even telling Diabolo he's coming, to tell him from now on they'd better not be seen together. And avoid calling each other. Cut off all ties, in fact. Not hang out with a bunch of Frenchies anymore. But Diabolo finds that pretty funny.

"Oh, I see, the closet. Y'know, I know all about that. I'll go there instead of you. Come on, I'll make you a Nespresso."

"I don't want a Nespresso!" Elias says. "Maybe you don't give a flying fuck about the police, but me, it's bugging me out of my mind, the judges and all that shit. I'm outta here. And don't call me anymore, please, Diabo. Never again until it's over. Ciao."

As he's leaving, he walks by Dina Aziza, who's coming out of her room in bare feet and a black bra and matching sweatpants, still jet-lagged, it would seem, and he stops to look at her. Even more beautiful in real life than in a photo. Gracefully muscular, satin skin, almond-shaped green eyes—in short, a wonder. She smiles at him furtively and goes to make coffee at the machine. Diabolo goes over to her like a landlord, nonchalant but possessive, and gives her a long kiss on the neck. She smiles at him nicely but looks at him in such a way that he does not go on. Then he walks Elias down to the street.

"Dina and me, it's a done deal," he claims.

"Ah, very good, mazel tov. She's very beautiful."

"Yeah, and she's crazy about me, which doesn't hurt," Diabolo brags.

"You're not going to call me again, even once, agreed?"

"If that's what you want, bro," the big man sighs. "But I'll miss you. Send me messages through Jérémie, my lawyer."

"OK."

"Or through Manu."

"What about the battery? Where is it?" Manu asks Romy.

"It was stolen, that's the problem," Romy answers without being taken aback in the least.

"Yeah but look, an electric bike with no battery, that doesn't interest me, really."

"So buy one."

"You kidding? A battery's at least two thousand shekels!"

126

"Oh! Stop complaining already, you're giving me a headache!"

"I'm not complaining, I want something for my money, that's all."

"I'm sick of you! I can't stand you anymore!" she shouts and walks away to shut herself in the bedroom, slamming the door and leaving him standing in the living room with the bike.

Shaken by this new explosion from Romy, poor Manu pedals off without a murmur with only his legs for a motor. What a swindler! What a thief! How can he still be desperately in love with her? She is so horrible. He pedals with his tongue hanging out and his head wobbling: without a battery, an electric bike is just a dead weight. He stops at the bike store at the corner of Ben Yehuda and Arlozorov.

"How many installments do you want to pay in?" the guy asks.

"Ten, is that possible?"

"In Israel, everything is possible," the shopkeeper answers with a big smile as he takes his credit card. "But do you have a good lock?"

"No, now that I think of it, she didn't give me one," Manu admits.

"Without a lock, it'll be stolen right away."

"Really?"

"You bet. Take this Kryptonite. It's the strongest, you'll see."

"But how much does it cost?"

"Four hundred and eighty shekels."

Luckily, the electric bike gives him an intoxicating feeling of freedom, because otherwise, it's ruinous. That is, when Romy's the seller, it costs an arm and a leg, or the eyes in your head. Speaking of eyes, the ophthalmologists at Ichilov Hospital finally took off his dressing. Now Manu wears glasses with smoked lenses. But he can't see much out of the damaged eye. Just movements, moving shadows. And driving with one eye isn't easy. All in all, six thousand shekels for this old wreck, it's really sickening, isn't it? And with two totally smooth tires, to take the cake! He hadn't noticed Romy's last act of treachery. She really had him there.

But could he have refused? She's got him by the balls, it's horrible.

# CHAPTER 18

Elias goes home to rest and wait for Olga. He lies down on the couch with his eyes half-shut. The phone rings just as he's falling asleep. Elias sits up with a start; he doesn't know the number on the screen, but he picks up, afraid the cops are calling back already.

"I believe the criminal theory in your case," Amos Kirzenbaum, the blogger at *Tag Shalom* with an identical name to the main character in his novel, announces immediately.

"So do the cops."

"Yes but according to me, you're the guilty party."

"How's that?"

"You sold them the car, and you went to lift it in the middle of the night."

"You see my file, or what?"

"No, no . . . well, yes, no, yes, that's my business."

"It's not really your business, and the police are the ones investigating. You should wait until they've finished," Elias calmly advises.

"Second question: Why didn't they talk about it on H24?"

"They did talk about it."

"No, not in the headlines."

"I can give you the editor-in-chief's number if you wish. Ask him why."

"OK, I'll look into it."

That's all, this time. Not displeased to have kept his cool, Elias gets up and pours himself a glass of Merlot. Moreover, it's the first time since this business started that he finds himself doing pretty well in a delicate situation. Good self-control, emotions in check. As for the real Kirzenbaum, like the one in his novel, he can't stand him. Maybe that's why his book isn't going anywhere. Nothing's harder to write about than a character you don't like. In any case, he didn't show him his abhorrence during that phone conversation, and at least that's something. Not the slightest aggression or paranoia.

He feels a certain serenity, or rather a certain fatalism, and begins to whistle a tune. But he sees Juliette staring up at him from her balcony down below, and the torment starts up again. That woman! When will she let go of him, for godsake? Will he have to move again so as not to have her after his ass? The telephone rings again, Marcel this time.

"The Netivot cops called me, Elias. You might have told me the Shabak had reclassified . . ."

"Shows I was right not to make a flap about it. We would've looked smart, claiming it was a terrorist attack."

"Yes, but after all, they asked me some embarrassing questions about the time you brought back the car."

"Why embarrassing? I came back at night like I always do, and I brought the car back to the car guys the next day since it was misfiring all the time."

"Yes, but what did you do with the car during the evening?"

"What did you expect me to do with it? I parked it in my stall in the basement."

"Usually you bring it back to the garage."

"No, I always keep it in my stall."

"All right, OK . . . so you went to the cops in Netivot today?"

"Yes."

"So you weren't sick."

"Yes, I was sick, but I went there anyway. I even threw up in the street."

"And you're better now?"

"I'm resting."

"You think you'll come in tomorrow?"

"I hope so."

That was tricky, too, and yet Elias remained the master of his nerves. He didn't raise his voice or give in to panic.

Basically, this situation is becoming really instructive, teaching him not to be a slave to his urges, to his intrinsic violent tendencies. It's helping him get out of his prolonged adolescence, despite the actual threat hanging over him. His intelligence is doing the rest. All he has to do is cut off contact with Diabolo for his version of the facts to stand up. At worst, even if they finally establish the connection between them, they can't accuse him of having sold the car and stolen it from the Bedouins. They'll have to choose between one of those accusations. The Bedouins will have to admit the man who sold them the car is not the same as the one who stole it back. Of course, if they follow through with the investigation, they'll discover he and Diabolo were accomplices. But if they do charge him, isn't it better to be two in the dock rather than all alone?

If only it were just a question of logic! Unfortunately, it's quite likely those two guys will pay dearly, and his guilt when he thinks of them still hasn't dissipated. On the contrary. But he still hasn't found a way to clear them without condemning himself at the same time.

Manu calls to suggest a hookah and they meet at Yafo. But they leave the hookah place without even a puff because Diabolo's there, too, with Dina, in front of a narghile. So they go to Par Derrière, which moved from King George Street into a place that looks like a hacienda facing Olga's. She joins them an hour later, and all three of them have dinner there. The new menu at Par Derrière is still more appetizing than the old one, particularly its stunning raviolis with truffles, while the wine list has a Saint-Estèphe at a hundred shekels for a glass that cannot be refused—or accepted, because as far as the six-hundred-shekel bottle goes, with an Israeli salary all you can do is dream about it.

"Mind you, when someone sells you a used bike for six thousand bucks . . . ," Manu notes, to put the price of the red in perspective.

"Six thousand!" Elias shudders.

"Well, yeah, add a battery, two tires, and a Kryptonite to the starting price, just add it up."

"Poor Manu, she really took you to the cleaners!"

Olga points out that a swindle involving a vehicle is a common point in both their affairs, and Elias gapes at her.

"Why're you saying that, honey? Mine is an attempted assassination. Why're you talking about a swindle?"

"Because . . ." Olga begins haltingly. "Because even if I thought about it all day, I couldn't see why those two Bedouins would want to assassinate you if they're not terrorists and you didn't swindle them."

They look at each other in silence as if they weren't madly in love anymore. As if they hadn't committed the rest of their lives to each other, for better or for worse, before the whole newsroom. So Manu doesn't know where to look. Extremely embarrassed, he gets up mumbling, "Excuse me, I'm going to take a piss again, must be my prostate."

Olga takes Elias's hand in her own. "Darling, I'm with you," she says again. "Trust me, please. Believe in us. We'll get out of this. We'll find a solution."

"But you're talking to me like that asshole Kirzenbaum! How can you do that?"

"Let me deal with that guy," she says. "I'm going to smash him to smithereens, I swear. I'll knock him down and drag him out feet first. Just stop lying to me. Please, honey."

Where does she get chutzpah like that? A girl of twenty-five, a reporter for only six months, and not even! Suddenly Elias no longer looks at her with the same lover's eyes. She no longer makes him think of the Jew in Proust with "a slight mind" but a blonde with a very sharp mind; cutting, in fact, an extremely special intelligence—very feminine, intuitive, and practical, but capable of putting things together.

They go up to her place, and Elias finally breaks down and confesses. He tells her the whole story in detail, minus the quickie with the jeweler on Dizengoff Avenue. Anyway, what importance can it have, a lay in a moment of melancholy? In his eyes, it doesn't count any more than if he had just held the door open for the lady, except that Olga wants them to go there together to get a reimbursement for the jewel. For her, it's essential to recover that money, even if it means getting less than what Elias paid for it. And above all, give it back to the family of the two Bedouins for the lawyer's fees they're going to need.

"Might as well confess to the cops," Elias answers without losing his calm.

"Yes, that's true," Olga finally admits. "But we do have to give them back that money one way or another. That's the starting point, I'm sure of it."

"Not before this business is over."

"Yes, before! And then a piece of jewelry worth twenty thousand shekels at Elkaïm's for a new immigrant with your salary—it's suspicious. Suppose they search your place . . ."

"They won't!"

"How d'you know?"

Elias finally manages to return to the jeweler's alone. While the jeweler is all smiles and honey when she sees him come in and excitedly locks the door and deactivates the alarm to drag him into the back, already lifting her skirt, she sends him packing when he asks her to reimburse the jewel.

"You here to screw me or bug me?"

"You've got to understand, I messed up, and I need money," says Elias in Hebrew, trying to cajole her.

"Buzz off, or I'll ring the alarm!"

"Look, you can still—"

"I'm counting to three." And Elias drops it. All he needs is for her to call the cops.

"I'll give you five thousand shekels for it, not one more," she says.

"Go to hell!"

"You'd rather I ring the alarm?"

"So go ahead," he answers bravely.

"OK, I'll give you seven thousand," she says, provided he humps her.

This time Elias accepts, knowing he'll have to dig deep in his mental resources to get a hard-on again with this old sow. So he says, "OK, raise your skirt," but she actually lifts it above her waist, revealing her whitish, wrinkled thighs. Still, he manages to stuff it into her for two to three minutes, thinking of Sandy with her mouth full of salad, Juliette in her little sarong, this one, that one, even a certain Miss World 1999 in a special Christmas issue of *Playboy*, and finally he walks out with a stack of crunchy two-hundred-shekel bills in his pocket.

Then he gets an alarmed text from Olga, informing him that Kirzenbaum has published an article in English on his blog. Elias connects right away. He's aghast to discover a story titled "Terrorist Attack or Racket?" illustrated by a photo of himself taken from Facebook. Everything is related quite exactly, including the mechanism of the swindle, but the pro-Palestinian blogger still knows nothing about Diabolo, except that he is, it seems, "a sinister-looking obese man."

# CHAPTER 19

Ever since Elias confessed the whole affair to her, Olga is in a state she's never known before. Boys do crazy things for her, sure. There were others. Lots, even. She's so pretty! But now there's a veritable tragedy, and she is the cause. With frightful repercussions for lots of people. But Olga is aware that if there's any chance of saving Elias and their relationship, she'll have to discredit Kirzenbaum. She just has to get into the skin of the kind of woman she is not, a Mata Hari or a simple sexy teaser who can lure an enemy of the male sex into a trap. She also knows she's on the wrong side of the truth, and that torments her. But she's made her choice: between Elias and the truth, she's choosing Elias: Elias over justice, Elias over truth, Elias over everything. The complete opposite of what she was taught in journalism school. But do you learn to deal with torment like this in the course of those studies? With falling head over heels in love like she is?

During this time, the atmosphere of the H24 newsroom has become electric. All the computers are connected to Kirzenbaum's blog, and when Elias comes in around three, Marcel takes him aside in a locked office, where the megadirector and the gigadirector of the channel are waiting for him.

"Tell us what happened," Marcel asks him. "We can't have a journalist in our editorial offices who's in trouble with the law."

"But I'm not in trouble with the law," Elias answers. "I was the victim of an attempted murder, and on the pretext that a blogger on *Tag Shalom* voices a doubt, there you go! You accuse me of I don't even know what, exactly. My own employer . . . that's pretty far out! After wanting to turn me into a hero instead of defending me . . . at least admit I'm the one who didn't want to exploit the event, whereas you wanted to make a whole megillah out of it!"

"Yes, OK," the gigadirector admits, "but did you or did you not sell the channel's car to those poor Bedouins and then take it back?"

"Never in my life!"

"Isn't a very fat man one of your friends?"

"More than one, even. So what?"

"Well, because according to the article, a big fat man is the one who stole their car in the middle of the night."

"There's the proof it's not me!"

"Yes, but according to the paper," the megadirector insists, "he could be your accomplice."

"Insinuations!"

"In any case, for the moment," Marcel announces, "you can't work as a journalist anymore."

"That's revolting!"

"You'll go into production," the gigadirector announces. "You know enough about technique, right? So one week of training and then you're in charge there. Until we get to the bottom of this business."

# CHAPTER 20

They have an appointment in one of the twin cafés in front of the Habima Theater, but Olga is so nervous that at the last moment she can't remember if it's the one to the right or the left. She's sorry she didn't ask him to meet at the Café Français, instead of this place, the best spot in Tel Aviv to miss each other when you're going to have a drink with someone whose face you don't even know and you detest in advance. So she sits down at random on the terrace of the one to the left facing the theater. Kirzenbaum appears a little later in a shapeless jacket, extremely annoyed, saying no, it was the one to the right where they were supposed to meet, and it's not very nice not to give a damn about the agreed-upon spot. This negotiation's off to a good start! But then she senses she's making an impression on him, with her clingy little gray silk suit and her beautiful blonde hair loose on her shoulders. He's impossible to describe.

Medium height, medium-long hair, nearsighted, age uncertain, toneless voice . . .

"Can I see?" he asks without waiting, and Olga puts the thing under his eyes. "Where'd you get this photo?" he asks distrustfully.

"That, I won't tell you until we agree on a price."

"What price?"

"Fifty thousand shekels," Olga says coldly.

"You're kidding!"

"Exclusive rights, of course."

"Still!"

"Take it or leave it."

*What's this pretty chick playing at, calling herself a* Tag Shalom *sympathizer but probably a Ukrainian whore?* Kirzenbaum wonders. Certainly a Ukrainian whore despite her French accent. It's not even a scoop, this photo, nor an affair making the headlines, just a piece of evidence to illustrate a pseudoinvestigative story like the ones he regularly writes against the Israeli army.

"I can't even give you ten percent of that," he confesses.

"Too bad," Olga answers, taking back the photo. She slips it into her purse and gets up. But Kirzenbaum grabs her by the wrist and forces her to sit down.

"Wait a second, please. You didn't even tell me who's who in this photo. Well, yes, I recognize the reporter from H24, but the other fat guy, there? Can I take a look at his face?"

She puts it in front of his nose for a few seconds before putting it back in her purse and getting up again to leave.

"Wait, wait, what's his name, his accomplice?"

"Gérard Valensi, or Diabolo, if you'd rather."

"And what's your connection to Elias Benzaquen?"

"I'm his ex. I'm the one who took the picture. The bastard threw me over, and I want to make him pay."

"The moron! Pearls before swine! A gorgeous girl like you . . . alone now, huh? Because I can . . . would you like to go to the movies tonight, the Cinematheque is having a retrospective of . . . um . . . the other idiot who became a rabbi, I have tickets . . ."

"Fifty thousand shekels or nothing," Olga interrupts him, putting her smartphone to her ear to pretend she has someone at the other end of the line.

"If you're really a *Tag Shalom* sympathizer, you should give it to me for free."

"I'm a whore, you dope!" replies Olga, putting the phone back in her purse. "Don't you get it?"

"Give it to me!"

"Let go of me!" she shouts, loud enough to alert the passersby.

Kirzenbaum immediately takes two steps back, raising his arms like in a Western, but he keeps walking behind her with his hands up, afraid of being accused of harassment. They walk up Rothschild Boulevard like that, among the joggers and roller skaters on the central pathway, up to the first stand where Olga stops to drink a Limonana. Still with his hands up, Kirzenbaum asks the bartender for a strong espresso, "with the sugar already stirred in, please." The bartender gives him a funny look, with a half smile on his lips as if he thought it was a sketch on *Candid Camera*.

"OK, put your hands down," Olga finally says to him in English, and Kirzenbaum lowers his hands.

"You gotta realize we're not rolling in dough at *Tag Shalom*," he whimpers. "We don't have money. Not a cent! It's pure poverty, I'm telling you."

"What about the subsidies from the European Union?"

"Excuse me?"

"A hundred thousand euros a year, that's not nothing."

"But that hardly covers expenses! We've got observers everywhere, you don't realize what that costs, the volunteers' little cameras! Not to mention thefts from volunteers . . . they may be volunteers, but they steal us blind anyway. Well, the Occupation is terrible, I swear, but . . ."

"OK, so let's say thirty thousand shekels."

"Ten thousand, no more," he says.

"Twenty thousand, my last offer, take it or leave it," Olga concludes. "My place at seven thirty for the exchange. Twenty thou' in cash, got it?"

She walks back up Rothschild Boulevard alone, quite pleased with herself for hooking Kirzenbaum. Now he has to bite on the hook and post the photomontage she made. You can see an obese man next to Elias, leaning on a four-wheel drive Subaru, the same model Elias sold the Bedouins but red instead of white. Naturally, the fat man is not Diabolo. Olga found his picture in Google images. With his bleach-blond hair and rosy complexion, he looks more like an Austrian tourist in some Asiatic sex paradise than a plump, dark Sephardi like Diabolo. Olga replaced the landscape of sand and sea with a stony landscape like the Negev's, and her montage really creates the illusion. Let's hope Kirzenbaum, blinded by his desire to get Elias, lets himself get trapped.

Olga also senses the blogger is one of those men who'd eat out of her hand, and so smarmy, such a whiner, that he makes her feel like indulging in little sadistic pleasures. This business is getting exciting! What's more, Elias knows nothing about it. She did the whole thing secretly, alone with Photoshop.

As she crosses Allenby Street, she sees Manu at the counter of Japanika Sushi with a blonde girl she doesn't know, and she comes over to give him a little pat on the back. A bit surprised, even embarrassed, Manu introduces her to Juliette, and the two girls kiss each other as if it were perfectly normal. Besides, Olga still doesn't know who Juliette is. Elias has never mentioned her. Juliette, on the other hand . . . of course she knows her rival, and of course she'd recognize her anywhere. Her nonchalance, above all. That fascinates her. She would so like to be like Olga. Not give a damn about anything, at least on the face of it. As for Olga, while she doesn't envy anything about Juliette, she would like to get to know her, have a friendship, giggle together, build castles in the air, talk about boys, and shake her like a plum tree at the same time—in short, be her new girlfriend. Truly love at first sight.

"What do you do in Tel Aviv?"

"I sell paintings."

"You have a gallery?"

"It's not mine," Juliette says. "But yeah, I'm the one who does everything."

"Where?"

"Abarbanel Street. It's called—"

"Oh yeah, Moins de Mille, I know it. I love it. I'll drop by to see you, all right?"

"Umm, yes . . . when?"

"Anytime. Just like that!"

"OK, fine, yes," Juliette says, vaguely worried, but relieved, too, to discover Olga's a real person and so approachable, not just a silhouette.

Then Olga goes back to change. She puts on black jeans, ballet shoes, her tortoiseshell Ray-Bans, and leaves for work. She goes by the office to kiss Elias but doesn't say a word about her date with Kirzenbaum, just that she ran into Manu at the Japanika with someone named Juliette, "super pretty." Elias shudders. If only Manu could stop seeing his ex, dammit! But what does he see in her? You'd think he was doing it on purpose. Suddenly he asks himself, What if Manu was pretending to be crazy about Romy just to hide that he loves Juliette? A terrible theory for Elias, because that would be the end of their friendship. But it's not impossible. After all, that girl never knew her father and the age difference between her and Manu isn't a real obstacle. On the contrary, even. They could easily end up stirring up a Freudian stew between them.

But if Olga starts seeing her, too, that would be the last straw! As if he didn't have enough to bug him without adding a possible friendship between Olga and his ex . . . since they have different schedules, with Elias ending his day when Olga's starting hers, they agree to meet at his place on Levinsky Street around 10:00 p.m. That leaves a little time for Olga to prepare the rest of her plan. At seven, she's back home, and at seven thirty on the dot she hears the doorbell ring. But she doesn't answer right away. She waits until Kirzenbaum rings twice and lets a few more seconds go by before going to open the door for him. A humanitarian or not, a great moral conscience or not, he looks like a big pervert.

"Oh, it's you!" she says, feigning surprise.

"May I point out that we had an appointment," he replies, already vindictive but giving her a funny look, for she's totally changed style since this morning, wearing only a little mauve satin dressing gown that goes down no farther than her butt, and black high-heeled mules she bought half an hour ago at Derech Yafo in a store that sells accessories for Ukrainian

147

whores. It gets Kirzenbaum right away, but it also intimidates him. He sits down at the edge of the couch—prudently, you might say—while she drops down next to him with her legs crossed high and her thighs mostly bare.

"Did you bring the money?"

"Yes, yes, of course," he answers, tapping the pocket of his dull yellow-gray-brown jacket. He takes out the wad of bills and puts it in the little space still free between her and him in the hollow of the seat. Olga takes the money and slowly counts it while he eyes her body, visibly naked under the peignoir. Sensing he's devouring her with his eyes and he's not attentively following the count, she intentionally makes a mistake.

"I'm only finding fifteen thousand."

"Oh, hey! No!" he protests. "Count it again, the twenty thousand are there."

Olga gets a kick out of recounting out loud and laying the bills on his thigh one by one, right next to his fly. By the time she reaches the seventh bill Kirzenbaum has lost count. He is well aware that he's wrong to let himself get excited by this so-called Frenchwoman, but while he's a man who can fight against the Occupation, there's nothing he can do about his erections. He'd give his right arm to screw Olga. She's putting him in a state of rut he has never known. He's breathing hard without realizing it as he tries to quell the insurrection between his thighs.

"You're not feeling well?" she asks naively.

"Yes, yes, why do you ask?"

"You're puffing like a steam engine!"

"I'm fine."

She picks up the money slowly and gets up to get the photo. "You're really sexy!" he calls to her, with his tongue hanging out, and Olga turns around and looks him up and down for a moment, just a moment, for him to feel even more miserly, more milquetoast, more of a wet blanket than he is.

"Do you want something to drink?" she asks him then, coming back with what he's paid for.

"Oh yes, if you have something cold."

"A Nespresso?"

"Ah, well no, I wanted something cold, not hot . . . uh . . . and then coffee at night . . ."

"Yes, that's not good, and anyway I've got to go now, *motek*."

"So when do we see each other again?" he says as he gets up with his arms stretched out to try to grab her.

"Next week, if you have time for me," Olga simpers, avoiding his embrace.

"Before. Before that! I've got to see you before, OK? I've got to!" he shouts, at the end of his tether. "That is, if you can."

"Come on, don't act like a child!"

Once she's succeeded in getting him out of there, she can sink down on the sofa and breathe at last. A weight has fallen from her shoulders. She acted without thinking, but it's not so easy to morph into a femme fatale when you're a solid Savoyard woman from Chambéry who likes simple things like fondue and mountain streams. It's still less easy because she's managed her affair in secret, without saying a word to Elias. Just to save him. She is quite simply mad about her guy—she hadn't foreseen that either. Her great love, you know, the man of her life. While she landed in Tel Aviv for an unpaid internship, with no other goal than to enrich the little professional experience she had, she now sees herself with a ring on her finger. What's more, Marcel made her a salaried employee. It commits you, all that. The upward spiral of life. It's fascinating. Everything takes off all of a sudden, and there's no going back.

A merry-go-round of texts follows, each more lovestruck than the last. Kirzenbaum wants to see her again right away, in an hour, in a half hour, in a minute. She fingers the bills he left, reflecting on the best way to give them to the family of the two Bedouins. That's the next stage of her plan. But above all, to discredit Kirzenbaum by getting him to publish those photos. So she goes to the trouble of answering his messages with phony romantic platitudes like "Give me another week to be all yours," but she can't wait for the whole thing to be over with.

The other question is to find someone to join her when she goes to the encampment near Mitzpe Ramon to hand over the twenty-five thousand shekels. She doesn't feel up to going there alone. It can't be Elias, of course. Why not with Manu? He probably wouldn't refuse, but he's too close to Elias. And he doesn't speak Hebrew that well. Go there with her new girlfriend, Juliette—that would be perfect! Two girls are always better than a fake couple for this kind of trip. And then it would create a superstrong connection between them.

"Why d'you want her number?" asks Manu warily.

"No reason, I think she's cool."

"I'll ask her first, OK?"

But Olga goes straight to Juliette at the gallery on Abarbanel Street, claiming she wants to buy a painting she saw on Facebook, and in the same breath proposes they go on a little expedition. Olga gifts Juliette a bottle of Miss Dior her mother brought back from the Duty Free at Roissy-Charles de Gaulle the last time she came to visit her. Naturally, Juliette wonders what Olga's getting at and if buying the painting isn't just a pretext for God-knows-what scheme. Either Olga doesn't know she's Elias's ex, or this girl is the kind who likes to pal around with the exes. These things exist. But Juliette has to know and know fast, for this ambiguity is very disturbing. Hurtful, almost. If Olga knows what happened between her and Elias, and she's acting as if nothing happened, that would be pure sadism.

However, Juliette accepts the bottle of Miss Dior and even gives Olga a kiss to thank her.

"What're you doing this Shabbat, Ju?" Olga asks her, already at the nickname stage.

"Nothing special, probably sleep late and then the beach."

"Do you feel like going to Mitzpe Ramon with me?"

"To do what?"

"I don't know the Negev . . ." Olga suggests.

"Got a car?"

"I'll rent one."

"Well, why not?" says Juliette, a bit evasively.

"No, don't worry. I'll pay for everything."

How can she refuse? Olga has such a tender way of pushing to get what she wants! All she has to do is like the person to deploy all her charm, and she's liked Juliette from the start without even knowing why. Her delicacy, perhaps? Or the beauty mark on her right leg? Her beauty, so fresh? *Could she be a lesbian, by any chance?* Juliette wonders, without really believing it. Elias would never be infatuated with a lesbian. Or a bisexual. He only likes real females, she thinks. Strange, all that. But OK, she would have to talk to her, if they really become friends.

Time may do its work, but Juliette has not healed yet. Luckily, the gallery pretty much occupies her, at least when she is there. But the rest of the time her thoughts are entirely devoted to Elias, and the desire to knife him is rising inside her like a black tide. There are days when her suffering becomes so intense that, yes, she envisages it, she fantasizes, she sees herself surprising him at dusk on Levinsky Street like in a crime novel, stabbing him twenty times in the back. Then it goes away or dissolves into the activities of daily life. In two months, she has transfigured the Moins de Mille gallery. It used to be just a messy, glorified storage place, but it has turned into a showcase where all the bohemians in Tel Aviv come streaming through from morning to night. The young painters of the city all seek out Juliette now. Her calendar is chock-full of appointments. In a few weeks, she's become someone who's important here, both for artists and collectors, and her boss gave her a raise of a thousand shekels a month. Gallery owners on Ben Yehuda Street also call her with job offers, but for the moment she feels good in Florentin and doesn't feel like settling in the north of the city—too bourgeois. The provincial woman she was when she arrived, unhappy and upset, has become one of Tel Aviv's most sought-after figures in the art world to the point where she must often juggle multiple invitations for the same evening. That helps her forget Elias, too, except that they still live across from each other, a nagging reminder of her unhappy love affair.

In short, she agrees to accompany Olga to the Negev, but before Olga goes away, she does ask the question.

"Olga, do you know who I am, at least?"

"Of course, come on!"

"You sure?"

"Don't tell me you and Manu are dating."

"No, no, Manu's crazy about a certain Romy."

"The one with the bike, huh?"

"Right," Juliette answers, giggling. And in a rather cowardly way, she laughs with Olga at Manu's sentimental misfortunes instead of telling her she's Elias's ex. For now that she thinks of it, hiding the truth from Olga is the best way of getting close to Elias again. With her mind working at top speed, she sees all the advantages she could get from this friendship. How could Elias still reject her if she became Olga's closest friend?

And then when she's put things in order in her mind, she doesn't consider herself Elias's ex anymore, but his *tikkun*, an old hard-to-translate Hebrew word that roughly means the price to pay to expiate a misdeed. What misdeed? Aside from being born of an unknown father. As if that were her fault!

# CHAPTER 21

When Olga announces that she's spending an all-girls Shabbat in the Negev with her new friend Juliette and that she'll take advantage of the excursion to give the money back to the Bedouins, Elias grows very somber. Tel Aviv is so small! To make friends with her like that, and tell her about the Bedouin business, to boot!

At the same time, he can't tell her now, and only now, that he had a long relationship with Juliette. Too late, mate! Olga wouldn't understand why he hid something so important from her. In fact, why did he keep that relationship under wraps? After all, they've been dating for several months. That's a real relationship, not a passing roll in the hay. So why does he cultivate that fanatical taste for secrecy, which always gets him into inextricable situations? It makes him so damned annoyed at himself. He's pissed at himself for being so weird. But Elias isn't just weird. Not only. He's also a good guy, a super friend, a generous guy, romantic and cultivated. A lot of people like him the way he is. And he's better than anyone at being liked when he wants to be liked. Only, that's how it is, he has trouble inside him, a really dark twist, like a malaise from the depths of time.

Poor Elias, caught in another spiral.

"I've had it with your business with Juliette! Had it up to here, I tell you!"

"What business?" says Manu, when they meet at Flo 10.

"You're in love with her!"

"Bullshit!" Manu retorts. "I'm not going to turn my back when I see her, OK? She never did anything to hurt me."

"But spending Shabbat in the Negev with Olga! Do you have any idea what that means for me?"

"No, I don't," Manu admits.

"It means your fucking Juliette is going to screw up my thing with Olga!" Elias shouts. "If you didn't see her so much, she wouldn't even know Olga!" Elias continues to shout.

"It's your lies that'll screw up things with Olga," Manu calmly answers, getting up to leave.

"Stay, please, Manu."

"You're always saying we're a small world here," Manu continues as he sits down. "If I didn't introduce Olga to her, someone else would have. So either you accept she's in our world, or go screw yourself somewhere else!"

"You're talking to me like that, Manu? That's what it's like being your best friend?" Elias begins to sob. "But for godsake, why the hell can't you understand me? Why d'you keep sending me back to my neurosis?"

"It reminds me of *Thelma and Louise*. You see it?" Juliette says.

"No, but I know it's with Geena Davis, and I love her," Olga replies as they're driving in the Negev with their hair flying in the wind.

The beginning of spring is an ideal season for a road trip through this mineral desert. The temperature's mild, the sun's caressing them, and the atmosphere is exuberant. The slightest pebble has glimmers of silver, and the air is so pure you could almost hear it tinkle. Olga has done well, renting an Audi convertible for a song, thanks to loyalty points accumulated at car2go on her father's credit card; and then there's her playlist. To learn Hebrew, Olga listens to Israeli artists, especially Mosh Ben-Ari, first of all because she doesn't have the time to go to Hebrew immersion during the week, and then because when she constantly listens to the same song she manages to detach each word in the sentence and find its meaning with her Hebrew-French app. Now, Juliette translates "Ve'Er Shelo," and it's a pleasure for Olga to finally understand what still escaped her in her favorite song. So she's full of gratitude for Juliette.

"You know what, Ju? Well, I can feel we're going to be friends for life!" she says, turning contentedly toward Juliette, who gives her an affectionate smile, while in her head, she remains on guard.

"Hope so," she answers nonetheless.

"You must meet Elias! You'll love him," Olga adds naively, and all Juliette can do is bite her tongue, but Olga doesn't notice and keeps describing Elias as only a woman in love can describe the man she loves.

Irritated, Juliette finally interrupts her right in the middle of a sentence. "Do we have enough gas?"

"Don't worry, there's a gas station two miles down the road."

"You know Mitzpe Ramon is over twenty-six hundred feet high, and it's over a crater one thousand six hundred and forty feet deep?" Juliette continues like a Blue Guide to stop her going on about Elias.

"No, I didn't know, but the thing that really gets me about Elias is—"

"Can you imagine it used to have a polar climate, fifty million years ago?" Juliette interrupts again.

"We would've come in parkas," Olga giggles, pushing her with her elbow. "I'm a Savoyard from the mountains, so I'm not bothered by the cold."

As they leave Mitzpe Ramon, Olga hands over a map to reach the Bedouin encampment. Juliette immediately recognizes Elias's special handwriting, with its delicate letters like black silk thread, set next to each other in an orderly way, and that upsets her so much she can't manage to be a good copilot. So she lets Olga go past the fork with the trail they need to go on, and they're forced to go back to where they began. It's extremely annoying, but Olga doesn't take it badly at all.

"I love you, you're totally out of it," she says, giving her a little smack on the forehead.

"Forgive me, I was mostly looking at Elias's handwriting, that's why," Juliette answers honestly.

"How d'you know Elias is the one who drew this map?"

"Uh, well since we were talking about him just before, I mean . . . you see, I, um, was assuming. Sorry," Juliette stammers.

"Don't apologize, you crazy or what? You're incredibly intuitive, Juliette, I love it!"

But Olga does take the map into her hands and puts it on the steering wheel before starting up again about Elias. "Did I tell you Elias is working on a book? A big novel, you know. He already filled up dozens of folders with notes." And she begins to tell her Elias's story of Amos Kirzenbaum, the last Jew in Tel Aviv, but she interrupts herself often to look uneasily at the side of the road until she finds that half-hidden trail that goes off to the right to the encampment. Then the Audi goes into the rocky trail that leads to the Bedouins, stirring up eddies of opaque dust, when suddenly there's a white Toyota police car coming at them the other way. As there's no room for two vehicles, Olga has to go into reverse to let the cops go by, and she backs up all the way to the turnoff.

When they're alongside the girls, the two policemen get out of the car and lean on both doors of the Audi.

"Hello, ladies," says the older of the two. "May we know where you're going?"

"What's he saying?" Olga asks Juliette.

"We're visiting," Juliette answers in Hebrew.

"But what are you visiting? There's nothing to see around here."

"Can we talk English?" Olga intervenes in English. "I don't understand Hebrew."

"Ah, you're French?" the cop answers, also in English. "OK. What are you going to do up there?"

"Assist a Bedouin family," Olga answers firmly.

"Assist how?" the cop asks.

"With money," Olga replies.

"I thought you were visiting," the young cop intervenes in Hebrew.

"Well, yeah, since we don't know the area," Juliette retorts in Hebrew too. "It's an excuse to visit at the same time."

"What'd he say, Jul?" Olga says, worried. "What did you say?" she asks the cop in English.

"Show us this money," the young cop says, snapping his fingers unpleasantly.

Olga turns off the ignition and grabs the bag containing the two-hundred-shekel bills. She takes out the wad and gives it to the younger one.

"They know you, those Bedouins up there?" he asks, after glancing at the money.

"Not personally, no, but it's because they . … well, I mean they had problems, and *Tag Shalom* is helping them out financially," Olga explains in a voice that's not so firm anymore—quavering, in fact.

"What kind of problems?"

"They need a good lawyer, in fact, that's why—"

"You have your papers?" the old cop asks in Hebrew. As Olga sees Juliette getting out her ID card, she looks for her passport and unwillingly gives it to the policeman, trying to smile. What bad luck, this chance meeting!

The old one goes back to the car with the IDs, while his colleague stays next to the Audi with the money in his hands, now leaning on the passenger side of the windshield, looking at the girls without saying a word. You'd think he was trying to find something to get them for, something wrong with the car, no doubt, but as it's an impeccable rental, Olga doesn't worry about it. Unless he just wants to create a feeling of unease by his insistent, hostile look. Israeli cops are often unpleasant, a bit like the drivers of the Egged bus fleet, who drive at breakneck speeds in the middle of town and take off by slamming the door in passengers' faces. Not conciliatory at all, and real nitpickers with the slightest offender. The old policeman comes back with their IDs.

"You're a reporter at H24?" he asks Olga in English.

"Yes, I am . . . how do you know?" she asks, surprised.

"So you know Elias Benzaquen?" the cop continues.

"Umm, yes," Olga answers uneasily, beginning to panic. "How?"

"My . . . well, a colleague . . . just a colleague," Olga pretends, and Juliette can't help giving her an anxious look. Why's she lying, dammit? What shit is this girl getting her into here?

"What about you?" the young cop asks Juliette in Hebrew.

"I work in a gallery."

"No, but you know that guy?"

"I knew him," Juliette answers in Hebrew, knowing that Olga doesn't understand.

"And you're *finished* with him?" the cop says in a slightly smutty tone, playing on the verb *finish*, which, in Israeli slang, also means "to come."

"No, that's not it, but we—"

"Who are you, to him?"

"Someone he used to know."

"OK," says the old one. "Follow us."

"But why?" Olga protests. "We didn't do anything wrong!"

"Follow us, please. And don't try to escape. Can I trust you?"

Goodbye Paris, Shalom Tel Aviv

"Escape?" Olga retorts. "But we're not prisoners, as far as I know!"

"You are now under arrest, so do not try to get away from us. OK?"

"Right . . . OK," Olga answers feverishly, after a moment of hesitation.

The police get back into the white Toyota and start off in a wind of gravel, with their flashing red and blue lights on the roof, while Olga starts the engine of the Audi just behind them.

"Why did you tell them he was just a colleague?" Juliette finally manages to ask.

"Because I . . . well, you see . . . it's incredibly complicated!"

"Exactly what are you hiding from me? What the hell is that money? What trap are you dragging me into here?"

"Oh, look, a coyote!"

Juliette turns her head toward the animal slipping between the rocks, but she quickly returns to the embarrassing question.

"Olga, please! Answer me!"

"I swear it's not a trap, Jul! It's just that Elias had a big problem, and I wanted to help him."

"What problem?"

"You're mad at me, I can understand," she finally says to Juliette. "But I swear to God I didn't want to get you into hot water. You believe me, Jul? Say yes, please. I love you so much!"

Juliette takes out her tobacco and rolls herself a cigarette. "What is Elias's problem?" she asks coldly, determined to get a clear answer. "Tell me, or I'll never speak to you again!"

Olga is on the verge of tears. She pours out the whole story while gripping Juliette's hand, and Juliette doesn't miss a bit of it. She laps up every word. She expected almost anything except this story. She's shattered to hear the judicial spiral Elias got caught in with this business. So at last, *that*'s the cause of his odious behavior, she tells herself. Everything is clear now. Poor Elias! If only he confided in her instead of fleeing her and becoming so cruel! If only he had the humility and the frankness and the simplicity to ask for her help instead of playing the cynical seducer! Of course she would have sacrificed herself for him. A thousand times, even! But how could she have suspected he needed her so much?

Juliette's reading of the events is certainly highly personal.

Why not, after all? It's so consoling to see things in this light that casts events in a way that serves her needs.

"So that was it!" she mutters when Olga has ended the story. "If I'd only known."

"You couldn't have done a thing, believe me, Jul. It's all my fault, don't you see? Elias went off the deep end to give me that damn jewel."

"My God," Juliette goes on in a murmur. "And Manu told me nothing about it! Not a word! What a bastard!"

"You don't understand it's a secret, or what? He was bound to secrecy, Manu. And now you're bound to secrecy too! D'you swear to keep this to yourself?"

"Keep what to myself?"

"Understand me, I promised Elias I wouldn't tell you anything!"

"But why, God dammit?" Juliette protests, stretching her neck as if she's talking to heaven. "Why be so cruel? We spent almost a year together!"

"Who?" Olga asks, puzzled. "You and Manu?"

Juliette looks at her with a mixture of anger and affection, disarmed by her naivete.

That's when Olga finally realizes her good friend Juliette, her new girlfriend, the girlfriend she adores, is her man's ex—and not a passing ex but an ex who counts. Juliette understands that she has finally understood and lowers her head contritely, ashamedly even, for having played this game of misunderstandings for so long instead of being frank from the very start. Long sighs escape from both their chests at the same time, like a chorus of regrets. They drive along in silence behind the cops, but their thoughts about Elias still file by from one brain to another, from one heart to another. They drive without knowing where this business will lead them, even if they're fundamentally innocent. They drive, innocent and yet accomplices, victims and yet guilty, both of them, for keeping their little secrets.

When they get to the police station of Mitzpe Ramon, Olga hears a notification from *Tag Shalom* beep on her smartphone. She just has the time to see the photos on Kirzenbaum's blog, and when she sees the headline of the article, she sighs again, this time from relief; it reads "Overwhelming Evidence."

Then the cops confiscate their phones and put Olga and Juliette into separate rooms.

# CHAPTER 22

There's a beep from *Tag Shalom* on Elias's iPhone just as he's joining Manu and Yoni at Flo 10 for their traditional Saturday noon shakshoukas with lots of walnut bread. It's a quasi-sacred moment of the week. The three of them—sometimes more than three—meet to stuff themselves without saying a word until absolutely nothing is left on their plates and there's no reason to put their spotless plates into the dishwasher when they've mopped up with the bread.

Elias gives them a vague hello, absorbed by Kirzenbaum's blog, although he doesn't understand that weird, abnormal, sinister image, and he has no idea Olga and Juliette are being questioned by the Mitzpe Ramon cops at the same moment. He takes a screenshot anyway and shows it to the two others. The caption of the photo claims it's the Franco-Israeli reporter Elias Benzaquen and his accomplice, Gérard Valensi, known as Diabolo, with the car used in the crime.

"You got some pals!" Yoni says jovially.

"What is this bullshit?" Manu asks more seriously. "Who's the fat guy?"

"No idea. It's not the right car or the right big guy," Elias says. "Kirzenbaum's hounding me, but he really screwed up here."

He immediately sends the image to Marcel and all his colleagues at the station via the WhatsApp group he set up with Olga to announce their relationship. The first bright spot since this business exploded! Finally something going his way! Finally some good news—Kirzenbaum's monumental blunder.

"It's a montage, right?" Yoni asks.

"Certainly," Elias answers, squinting. Suddenly he cries out, "I got it! Olga's the one who gave him that! I'm sure of it! She promised to fuck him up! Man, do I love you . . . my Olga! My honey!"

The waitress brings their shakshoukas, still bubbling hot in their metal dishes, but they don't touch them right away as they're concentrating on the images.

"Call her!" Manu advises feverishly.

The phone rings at least ten times before someone picks up, but it's a man's gruff voice answering in Hebrew. "Mitzpe Ramon police, I'm listening."

Elias starts, but he instinctively understands that Olga's phone is in the hands of the cops and he answers in Hebrew, "I'm sorry, I hit the wrong number," and hangs up. Seeing the expression on his face, Manu and Yoni conclude the bright spot lasted a very short time.

Barely one minute. Just a minute of relief, a tiny little minute of good news, and here we go again into deep shit. The inexorable sequence of trouble and menace is beginning again.

"She's with the cops," he announces. "Manu, call Juliette, please, to check if they didn't have an accident." But the same gruff cop's voice answers Manu.

"OK, they've been nabbed," Elias concludes.

They don't even touch their shakshoukas. The events are taking a very bad turn now. The affair is getting ugly and worrisome. What with dirty linen and bad luck, the noose is tightening. Elias thinks once again of the Zweig novel *Beware of Pity.* The title sums up the situation so well. *Everything is in books,* he says to himself, *notably that absurd feeling of guilt that makes you throw yourself into the lion's jaws.* Going to give the Bedouins back the money he'd stolen from them—Olga certainly had good intentions. She has a good heart.

*But she hasn't read enough,* Elias tells himself again. His darling is too young, too charitable. Just imagining her locked in a cell makes Elias want to scream. His Olga in the slammer! An inconceivable reality, but it is his new reality. And her parents are coming in less than a week to be officially introduced to him, my God! Will she be out when they arrive? What can he possibly say to them if she's not released by then?

Elias doesn't feel like a shakshouka at all now, and neither does Manu, but Yoni's stomach is gurgling.

"Hey, it's not Yom Kippur, y'know," he says, soaking a big chunk of bread in the yellow of an egg while Manu and Elias are pensively staring at their bowls.

A text from Marcel comes in at that moment: *I'm puzzled,* the ed-in-chief prudently writes, while Danielle Godmiche ironizes, *Has the white car turned red?*

Despite this apparent beginning of a change in the situation at work, Elias can sense that from tomorrow on, they'll go in for the kill when they learn Olga is in police custody in Mitzpe Ramon, far from Tel Aviv. Even their closest friends, their most faithful allies, will change sides, there's no doubt about it. The channel's most glamorous couple mixed up in a criminal affair—they'll be shelved, or unemployed, both of them. To avoid this disaster, she has to be released before the next day, Sunday, when they go back to work. There's no use for Elias's burning millions of neurons a second to find a solution, he can't think when he doesn't really know what's going on. He doesn't have all the pieces of the puzzle, since he knows nothing of the twenty thousand shekels she extorted from Kirzenbaum. He still thinks she went to Mitzpe Ramon just with the money he got from the jeweler's on Dizengoff. But then, what would they both be stopped for? It can't be for possessing such a small sum. But if it's not for that, what for? Besides, he can't call the Mitzpe Ramon cops, not him. His implication in this business is too great. Why not Manu? Or better still, Danielle Godmiche. A journalist, that would do the trick. And no one's better than Danielle at worming information out of the people she interviews, but with the charm of a fairy. She'd know how to get the Mitzpe Ramon cops to spill the beans without seeming to.

While they wait for her to call back, Elias and Manu let their shakshoukas get cold, while Yoni's sopping up the last of his and beginning to eye theirs. Not that he doesn't give a damn about Olga and Juliette, it's just that anxiety doesn't take away his appetite.

"Take mine," Elias says to him, and Yoni doesn't wait to be asked twice. He pulls Elias's bowl across the table, and there we go, a second shakshouka. He gobbles it down as if nothing were happening.

Danielle finally calls back and confirms the bad news. Olga has been arrested, while Juliette may be released in the next few hours. Danielle also informs him that Olga was transporting twenty-seven thousand shekels in her purse and not seven thousand as he thought, and the money came from the NGO *Tag Shalom*.

"But the cops are waiting for the NGO to confirm they gave Olga the money before they decide what they're going to do with her. They also suspect her of lying about your relationship," she adds.

"Can you contact Kirzenbaum, please, Danielle?" asks Elias, with his back to the wall.

"Sure, I'll do it right away."

"Stop eating, Yoni! Shit!" he screams as he hangs up.

"What d'you want me to do, it'll get cold!"

"She needs a lawyer," Manu says.

"What's the law on pretrial detention in Israel?"

"No idea. Call Diabolo, he must know."

"You call him, OK? I cut off all connection with him."

"I'll be expecting you," Diabolo answers.

# CHAPTER 23

Elias and Manu are leaving for Kerem on electric bikes, while Yoni remains at Flo 10 to finish his second shakshouka—before attacking Manu's, no doubt. "I'll meet you there," he claims nonetheless.

Traffic's easy on Shabbat, and they get there in five minutes. Diabolo greets them with a big smile on the terrace, as if all this drama were perfectly ordinary. "Don't worry, Elias, we'll get the kid out of there," he says ingratiatingly as he pours coffee. Lovely Dina comes up to say hello and then goes to walk her dog on the beach, and now they're just guys in the sun.

"She still living with you?" Manu asks.

"We're living together," Diabolo claims. "In fact, I'll give you the scoop on the announcement: we're getting married in Rome at the beginning of June."

"Mazel tov," says Manu, "even if it's a load of crap."

But friendship with Diabolo demands that you go along with all his fabrications, or else you hurt him too much. It's a very subtle attitude, but at the same time it's just something to get used to. You must be indulgent. Diabolo has a boundless need for recognition, and all you have to do is go along with the idea that all women are mad about him in order to put up with him. Except that hardly has Dina left the terrace than they hear another woman calling from his bedroom: "Da-a-r-ling! My coffee, please!"

It catches Diabolo off guard, and it bothers him. He gets up immediately to quiet the importunate lady and then returns as if nothing had happened.

"My lawyer will be here soon," he announces. "It's really nice to see you again, Elias."

"And how about me, what am I, chopped liver?" Manu complains, to relax the atmosphere.

The three of them seeing each other again makes them slightly nostalgic for their trio before all this nonsense, when all they did was party and live it up.

Had it really been only two months ago? Things had been good. Princely evenings, karaoke evenings, with lots of liquor and girls. But Elias notices the box of Havanas has shrunk an awful lot since then, and he gets worried.

"Business OK, Diabo?"

"Brilliant, blessed be He," the fat man answers, not at all disconcerted. "We already have a million clicks a day on *IBN*, can you imagine?" And then changing the subject completely, "Hey, Manu, any news of Romy?"

"She's not doing so great."

"Tell us."

"Well, she had to have a back operation. She was in incredible pain."

"That's why she became so nasty, maybe," Diabolo jokes. "Like in the comic strip, you know. What's its name already?"

"Tiboudou or something like that, right?" Manu says. "Or Caribou?"

"Kirikou," Elias tells them.

"She have health insurance in Israel?"

"Yes, yes, she's got Maccabi, but there you are, for that operation doctors' fees went three thousand shekels over . . ."

"Don't tell me you're the one who paid!"

"Well . . ." says Manu, fatalistically.

A big blonde in curlers and a flowery peignoir comes out of Diabolo's bedroom and sinks onto his lap, all lovey-dovey.

"This is my friend Louisa, from Neufchâtel," he says, extremely embarrassed, while the dull blonde cuddles up against him, siphoning kisses on his neck, and not just little friendly pecks, right! No, hickeys rich in little moans and groans. "Please, darling, we're working now," Diabolo grumbles, pushing her away, first nicely and then brusquely so that she rolls up to the stairs. "I gave her my room," he claims in a low voice when she's left the terrace. Manu nods his head in understanding, as one does with Diabolo when he gets tangled up in his webs. Elias's phone rings at this moment. Danielle informs him that Kirzenbaum was in fact contacted by the Mitzpe Ramon police, but he denied having given any money to Olga. He just admitted he'd bought the photos he published for twenty thousand shekels.

"Did you tell him it was a photomontage?" Elias asks.

"No, I wanted to talk to you first. Do you want me to call him back and tell him?"

"Absolutely not! I'm the one who'll contact him; thanks, Danielle, you're a love."

"You're welcome, Eli. Keep me in the loop, I'm either home or at Banana Beach all day."

"Can you believe it, guys?" Elias says. "She got twenty thousand bucks for that montage? She's not brilliant, that chick? Answer me, OK?"

"Olga's the best," Manu recognizes.

"Crème de la crème," says Diabo, raising the ante. "But what montage are you talking about?" And Elias shows him.

"You see the red-faced blond guy in flashy Bermuda shorts? Well, that's you, Diabo!"

"She violated my right to privacy!" Diabolo jokes. "What is all this bullshit?"

Elias explains the maneuver to him and begins telling everything to Jérémie Azencot, Diabolo's lawyer, who's arrived in the meantime, with his fine face of a sleepy partygoer in a bad mood.

"Here, legal procedure is different from France," Jérémie says. "They work the American way. If Olga is charged, she must plead guilty, and then the defense negotiates a plea bargain with the judge."

"But she's guilty of nothing," Elias replies. "I'm the guilty party!"

"And me, too, to some extent," Diabolo adds.

"We'll see about that afterward. Don't mix things up, guys. Here she's been apprehended with a large sum of money of doubtful origin. Right?" Jérémie says, and the three others nod. "OK, so if we stick to that—and thanks for giving me a coffee before we go any further. Wow, Diabolo, your terrace is supercool!" he observes in the same breath, to break with his rather lawyerlike tone.

"Oh no, Jérémie. Does that mean she won't be released tonight?" Elias asks.

"She may be, or she may not be."

"Oh no! No, no, no," Elias howls. "I'll go off my rocker!"

"He's very much in love," Diabolo whispers into the lawyer's ear as he brings him an espresso.

"Got a spoon, or should I stir this with my dick?" says Jérémie, in a foul mood.

"It's coming, Counselor!" Diabolo answers attentively, handing him a spoon.

"So, OK, what do we do?" Elias asks. The lawyer's attitude is grating on his nerves.

"I'm calling the cops," Mr. Azencot announces, after finishing his coffee in one gulp. "Can I have another, Diabo? Thanks."

He takes out his phone, goes to his file of police stations, finds the number of the Mitzpe Ramon police in two seconds, and clicks on it. The conversation starts up in Hebrew. Jérémie introduces himself as Olga's and Juliette's lawyer and hears them confirm what he already knows. Manu, Diabo, and Elias are hanging on his every word, although Elias is the only one who understands all of what Jérémie is saying.

"To demonstrate that the provenance of the money is fraudulent, you must confront my clients with Mr. Kirzenbaum, who gave them the money. Now, you have simply questioned the main suspect in the affair on the telephone and taken him at his word, whereas you are keeping my clients in custody. I contest the equity of your investigation, and I am asking you to release both my clients immediately." Jérémie slaps his case down like cards in a poker game 150 miles away.

"You'll contest it before the judge," is all the policeman says, and Jérémie finally hangs up.

"Racing results: the file will be presented to the judge tomorrow morning asking to charge Olga or prolong her detention, and Juliette will be released before tonight. I asked that the hearing not be held before noon, so I have the time to get there tomorrow."

"I'm going crazy! Crazy!" Elias yelps.

"Let's calm down and turn our attention to Kirzenbaum instead," Diabolo suggests. "Got his number, Elias?"

"What are you going to do with it?" Jérémie asks, concerned.

"Send him my picture," Diabolo replies lightly.

"Cut the crap," the lawyer says. "Let's wait for tomorrow's hearing to decide. We'll fuck him up right after that."

# CHAPTER 24

Juliette is released around 4:00 p.m. and goes back to Tel Aviv on the first bus that leaves after Shabbat's over. She would rather return in the Audi they arrived in, exhausted but in great form, as people are after weekends, but now she's going back sad and worn out. She wasn't even able to say goodbye to Olga before leaving the police station. They didn't even let her wave to her, and that broke her heart. Just at the moment she was beginning to like her and find her so fresh and endearing!

Her phone rings for the first time as the bus is pulling into Tel Aviv through Avalon North, but she doesn't answer the unidentified caller. Then the second time, still with a hidden caller, around 10:45 p.m. when she's leaving Tachana Merkazit, followed by two quite sinister Sudanese, certainly in an aggravated state of rut, and then the third call, this time with Elias's name clearly shown on her old Sony as she gets to Levinsky Street.

"I saw the light on. You're back? They released you?"

"I just got back," she answers.

"What about Olga?"

"They're still detaining her, I think."

"What d'you mean, you *think*?" Elias says, vainly trying to stop himself from yelling.

"Why didn't you tell me you were in trouble with the police?" Juliette asks him point blank. "You think I wouldn't have been capable of helping you?"

"But . . . what are you talking about?" Elias retorts. "And helping me to do what? Would you stop trying to remake history all the time?"

"OK, too bad, I'm tired now. I'm going to bed, Elias. Good night."

"Wait, Juliette! Wait, will you?" Elias shouts into emptiness.

He looks at his phone for a moment, as actors do in scenes when someone hangs up on them, and then he goes down and knocks on her door. She doesn't answer, so he knocks with more force, he drums and bangs with all his strength until an alarmed neighbor opens up to see what's happening. Snug in bed, Juliette then hears the shouts on the landing and finally gets up to open the door. Elias stops yelling and enters his old place.

"What is this sadism? Why won't you say anything?"

"Exactly what do you want to know?"

"How you were arrested, for godsake, it's not so complicated!"

"On the way there, on the road, that's all," Juliette answers evasively. "We bumped into the cops, and then I didn't know what was going on, so naturally we contradicted each other, and then it got us into deep shit."

"In other words?"

"Well, they saw we weren't being clear, we had a lot of money in the car, then they went to look at their database, and then poor Olga began to lose it."

"What'd she say?"

"They saw she worked at H24, so they asked if she knew you, and she said he's just a colleague. And I couldn't stop myself from jumping with shock."

Elias slumps down on the seat with his head in his hands, indifferent to the cat, Jean-Pierre, nibbling on his jeans. "Oh no, no, no!" he repeats twenty times over, starting to sob. "I can't stand her being in prison because of me . . . Olga, you understand, she's the light of my life. If she isn't with me, I go out. Can you understand that, Juliette? Huh?"

Juliette lets him pour it all out while getting something to drink from the fridge, but she can't find much since she didn't stock up at AM:PM on Frenkel Street that Shabbat. She does find an old can of Goldstar and puts it on the low table between two glasses.

"If you knew all she did for me," Elias continues.

"What are you here for?" she finally asks him, trying to remain stiff, whereas she feels a soft abandonment taking hold of her.

"You have to understand me, Juliette, maybe what I'm asking you is cruel, but you're the last person who saw Olga, and I need you to tell me more. Tell me she doesn't blame me. Tell me she'll get out OK, because otherwise I'm gonna die," he says, holding his head in his hands still. "Snuffed out. Finished. Over. The guy's had it. Like an asshole. The end of the end of his tether."

"Why don't you give yourself up?" Juliette suggests, still apparently ice cold but ready to fall into his arms. "That would really ease your conscience, Elias."

With that, Elias raises his head, dumbfounded. With his eyes on hers, he repeats "Give myself up" several times, as you do when you want a word to lose its meaning so it's no more than a sound.

"You want me to go to jail and lose my job and the little I've earned."

"You'd rather other people pay for you? The Bedouins, Olga? Who else?"

"That's the way you see me?"

"I get up early tomorrow. I'd like to go back to bed."

"So go ahead!" he answers without budging, as if he has no intention of leaving. "Go ahead. Go to bed. I'll just keep sitting here."

Taken aback by the provocation, Juliette doesn't know what she should do now. How could she sleep with Elias in the same room, at arm's reach? He's so good at rubbing it in, right where it still hurts. That love, that desire, that urge she swept under the rug and kept contained for months like a gas, only asks to explode out of her. On the other hand, she can't imagine that the sincere pain he's feeling can be reconciled with the idea of finding himself in the same bed with her this evening. Not so fast! Not already, honestly! But why not? She's well aware that anything is possible with Elias, all the turnarounds and all the possibilities that are irreconcilable in principle, everything that can shock or even scandalize her, upset and even sicken her. Besides, would it be just, unjust, or totally disgusting for him to spend the night with her when Olga's locked up alone in a cell in Mitzpe Ramon? Disgusting for Olga, yes. But for her? She's suffered so much because of him! Doesn't he owe her some reparation?

The novelty is that now Juliette feels connected to Olga in a very tender way, a connection that should grow stronger in the future. A real girlfriend. Being arrested together—that's something you can't forget. It marks you and leaves traces, like surviving a war or a shipwreck. So there's nothing to be gotten from conventional morality, no solution to be hoped for from the usual rules that govern faithfulness.

Juliette goes back to bed and turns off the lamp, leaving Elias sitting there in the darkness. But an anguished sigh escapes her at the thought that Olga could see both of them in this room or learn about it one day. That would hurt her so much. It would just be horrible.

"Why're you sighing?" Elias asks in the blackness. "You're thinking of Olga?"

"Yes."

"And you're thinking what, exactly?"

"Nothing, let me sleep, please."

Hoping to fall asleep, she tries to empty her mind again, or something like empty it, drive out the parasitical thoughts at least, the desires and fantasies. It doesn't work. She's awake, it's nighttime, and Elias is there, within reach. She can practically hear him breathe. No use turning toward the wall, she can't fight against the desire that comes to her from behind, as he liked to do in Jeru at dawn in days gone by, before he'd cut out and not communicate with her at all for a few days. And then, she's sure he feels the same thing and has the same urge, despite his anguish and sorrow. In such moments, you'd like to be able to set everything right with the wave of a magic wand, have the memory of a goldfish and feel nothing, satisfy your urge without hurting anyone and without suffering, without memories and without consequences, thank you and goodbye.

When will he lose all decency and come slip into bed with her?

# Chapter 25

The next morning, he gets to work at eight thirty, although he doesn't begin until an hour later. He walks right into Marcel's office. Elias wants to get the editor-in-chief to take him back as a reporter, on the grounds that he's been unjustly set aside because of fake news. He demands to be reinstated without delay, and this, before they learn Olga is in police custody. As she starts at 3:00 p.m. on Sundays, Elias hopes to create an irreversible situation if he can succeed before they realize his darling is absent and, in fact, being held by the cops. But Marcel already knows about it and says to him coldly, "Let's wait till Olga is released, OK? Did you get a lawyer to defend her?"

Elias stalks out of the office, slamming the door in disgust, and goes back to his workstation in production. At each limp handshake from a colleague, he feels still more abandoned. Only Danielle Godmiche gives him an effusive hug. He goes into a corner and calls Diabolo. "We're on our way," the fat man announces. "Jérémie's going to bring your honey back to you. Don't get all worked up!" That's what's great about hoods. They don't spare themselves, they don't judge or pre-judge, they're always ready to give you the air you need to breathe, the ten cents change to make a round number. Tel Aviv to Mitzpe Ramon in a Cinquecento—even if it's custom-ized and air-conditioned, that's really something when you're not obliged to do it! But Diabo doesn't have to be from nobility to have noble feelings. His ugly excess weight doesn't prevent him from being an aristo of the heart.

Waiting for Jérémie to come out of the court with Olga, he remains calmly in the car, puffing on a Cohiba while listening to the complete songs of Michel Sardou.

. "Your honor, we arrested Miss Olga Picard here in posses-sion of a large sum of money, which she justified by claiming it was a gift from the NGO *Tag Shalom* for the Khaldun fam-ily," the police officer in charge of the case begins before the impassive magistrate in Mitzpe Ramon. "We also found the defendant was lying about her personal relationship to Elias Benzaquen, who is involved in a criminal case against two members of the Khaldun family."

The cop's goal is to obtain an extension of the pretrial detention to have the time to show the connection between this money and the case of the two Bedouins, but especially the personal relationship between Olga and Elias. So he talks about factors that tend to prove there is an "attempt to suborn witnesses"—so he's already into big words—and his presentation does not neglect a single detail of the affair, while Olga listens attentively to the simultaneous translation as she sits in the defendant's place to the left of the judge. She has on the same clothes as the day before, the same makeup, and nonetheless the same freshness despite twenty-four hours in detention without being able to wash or even brush her teeth. She's a gem, that girl: grace incarnate in the clutches of the law. Jérémie was able to talk with her five minutes before the hearing, and he found her really top notch but also extremely detached, strangely distant, almost as if she were reporting in the court and not suspected of serious crimes. Not personally involved, you might say: a journalist to the core, not a criminal facing trial. He asked two or three questions about the circumstances of her arrest, and she answered precisely, although she seemed more interested in the little love note Elias had given him for her than in his strategy as a lawyer. A love letter in which her lover asks her forgiveness for letting her go on that wretched expedition and promises that when she gets back, they'll both go to Venice for a few days to forget all this.

When the cop has finished, the lawyer stands up to address the judge. "Your honor," Jérémie declares, "my client has committed neither a crime nor a misdemeanor, there is no Israeli law making it illegal to transport the sum of money she is accused of transporting. So we don't understand what the officer is getting at. Keeping her in detention brings nothing to the investigation, because every part of the case is already known. Moreover, Olga is ready to confront the generous donor who gave her this money, but the police did not wish to disturb that gentleman. Besides, my client has all the guarantees necessary for her to be released: no record, a salary, and a stable job. Therefore, I am asking the court to reject the police's request."

But the judge refuses to release Olga. She grants the police three supplementary days in detention, and the hearing is adjourned.

Jérémie joins Diabolo in the Cinquecento, and they leave empty handed for Tel Aviv. Diabolo is disappointed, but Jérémie really takes it badly. He could see himself already, swaggering around, freeing the beautiful captive in two shakes of a lamb's tail, and dining with her that same evening at the Cantina or the Brasserie on Ibn Gabirol.

"Now I can stick my finger up my ass!"

"She's Elias's chick, you don't have a chance. Even I can't . . ." Diabolo begins.

"Even you what?" retorts Jérémie, annoyed.

"You know very well no woman can resist me . . . hey, speak of the devil."

"The news isn't very good," Diabolo says. "They're holding her three more days. But take it easy, the cops don't have a thing on her, and Jérémie fought like a lion. You should've seen him. They were trembling in the corridors, I tell you. That is, there are no corridors in Mitzpe Ramon, it's just an image, but man, he's got the gift of the gab, I swear."

"I'm gonna die!" Elias howls.

"We'll get her Thursday."

"I'm gonna die!"

"Not before Thursday, please," Diabolo says.

"Tell him I'm going to sue Kirzenbaum for slander," Jérémie whispers.

"Hear that, Elias? Jérémie's going to fuck Kiki with a slan—"

But Elias has already hung up and didn't hear the joke. Olga's scheme didn't improve the situation, only made it worse: despite the publication of the fake, she's still in jail, and he's still more marginalized at H24, whereas Kirzenbaum can take it easy as he does his blog. It really makes you believe in pre-destination, in *fatum* as the ancients called it, in misfortune already written up above. For even an act of love like Olga's to have such perverse, devastating effects, you have to believe you're cursed.

He makes blunders all morning; his mind isn't in it. He distractedly works his console without thinking of what he's doing: close-ups that last a whole minute during a discussion, the camera focused on a participant who's listening while picking his nose while the speaker isn't even in the frame. Marcel finally charges into the production room to see what's going on.

"You're totally going off the rails, Elias."

"A forger accuses me, and you take his side! Olga's in the slammer, and you don't even ask the embassy to intervene! Just what are you waiting for? For us to kiss our ass goodbye, her and me? You want us dead? Is that it?" Elias retorts, aware he's risking everything.

For this could turn out badly; he might actually be thrown out after making a scene like this, it's possible. But it's also a good way of shaking up his colleagues, forcing people to take sides. Elias knows how to create divisions.

Danielle Godmiche finally says, "After all, we can't let them publish bullshit about Elias without reacting, Marcel. His honor is also the honor of the channel."

"Our lawyer is on it," Marcel protests.

"Yes, but meanwhile, Elias is being punished on the basis of a fake, and that's not right," someone else says.

"What's more, we're doing a blackout on Olga!" a third one chimes in.

"OK, OK," Marcel answers, sensing a growing rebellion. "I promise I'll clarify the situation before tonight. Meanwhile, I'll take it on myself to put Elias back in the newsroom."

The tension drops then, and Elias tastes a bit of inner peace at last. And yet Marcel knows the case inside out. He knows it's not so simple and Elias and Olga are not entirely blameless. But you have to save the store and face up if the machine is to continue to work. Luckily, for the moment, the Israeli media outlets aren't interested in the story. That gives him elbow room. Even Kirzenbaum has dropped it, no doubt afraid of being accused in his turn.

After work, Elias rushes to Kerem without taking any precautions. He's avid to hear about Olga, and Diabolo doesn't wait to be asked. He pretends he was at the hearing and embellishes the scene as much as possible. Inventing, making up stories, faking it to make someone happy—that's his thing, Diabolo. No need to push him.

"Y'know, she was fantastic on the stand, with the beautiful way she holds her head and her braided hair. Believe me, you're lucky to have a chick like that. She spotted me from far away, and she made a heart with both hands for me to take a message, and she wrote, 'Elias, I love you' with a marker on a piece of paper. The judge even asked her to be more discreet, you get the atmosphere, but it's wild, she's got you under her skin, trust me. And you should've seen Jérémie, he was perfect, he's a real mensch, believe you me."

"I hope he's not too expensive. I'm afraid to talk about bread with him."

"Cool it, we'll owe him, that's all."

"I feel like throwing a Frisbee," Elias says suddenly.

"Frisbee, now there's something new."

"Come on, we'll go to the beach and play a little game."

They walk to Banana Beach, which is next door, with Diabolo dragging his massive body along and Elias charging ahead. On Sunday afternoon, there are few people on the sand, and it's the best time to play, just before sunset. It sure is a change from Paris, nine miles of beach available all year round. It's even disproportionately long for a city like Tel Aviv, but above all it has an almost magnetic pull on French immigrants: you see them walking or biking up and down the Tayelet, not out of necessity, but just to take a look at the Banana Café to see if anybody's hanging out there, like when you're a teenager or on vacation, or like reminiscences of North Africa in times gone by, Khereddine and El Marsa, the Mediterranean, the dark skin of the girls and your buddies. Banana Beach is one of the last beaches of Tel Aviv before Yafo. It comes before Blue Bird, the surfers' beach, and it's recognizable not only by the green deck chairs and yellow beach umbrellas, but also by its bands of newly arrived French women and men of all ages. You can also find lots of French on Gordon Beach in the other direction, toward the north, where the developments on the Tayelet strangely make you think of a Hopper painting, God knows why, given the lathed promenades of the flooring and the smooth stone benches. It probably has to do with their geometry or design—who knows exactly why—but anyway, Elias is ready to throw the Frisbee when he gets a selfie from Juliette with little pink hearts and his urge to play immediately drains from him in a mixture of discouragement, shame, and remorse. Then a second message, just one word: *Tonight?* She wants to start again, it's clear, doesn't want to admit he was just momentarily distraught last night; it was a fit of passing madness like the time before, due to his anguish at being deprived of Olga. So Elias sits down on the sand, without feeling like playing at all, cursing himself and asking why he lets himself be ruled by his dick. And why did he screw her without a condom?

Not too unhappy that the game ended before it began, Diabolo comes up to him, slightly worried to see him in this state.

"Bad news?" he asks soberly.

"I'm so fucking sick of my screwups, Diabo . . . so sick, you know . . ."

"Don't torture yourself, it'll be OK. It always is."

"Help me, Gérard, I'm running right into a wall. Please give me some advice."

"What's your latest fuckup?"

"I slept with Juliette last night."

"Now there, you've got the rights to a Gold Card," Diabolo says, lightly.

"Without a condom."

"Let's go have a drink."

At this moment, a trio of malcontents charge out of the Banana Café with mean looks on their faces, full of frontal aggressivity toward Diabolo. They're young guys he hired as reporters at *IBN* despite their uncertain French, but he hasn't paid them for the month, as the coffers are more or less empty.

Diabolo's prosperous period is no more, as Elias realized when he saw the box of Havanas reduced to its starkest state the night before. *IBN* hasn't earned a thing up to now and costs more than it was supposed to, but these three little guys don't give a good goddamn. And they're mad as hell. Usually so full of respect for the boss, so solicitous, here they are with daggers drawn. Because they could already see themselves as star reporters, these guys—PPDA, FOG, BHL, their names contracted into universally known acronyms—and they believed so much in Diabo as a great media magnate! Great is their disillusion, strong is their bitterness.

"I want my money!" says one.

"You owe us!" the other says, rubbing his thumb against his forefinger.

"OK, guys," Diabolo replies. "I had a little cash flow problem, but it'll be settled next week."

"What day?" the third asks.

"Monday or Tuesday," Diabolo answers. "Here's a thousand bucks each, and the rest next week. But don't forget the refresher session Friday morning."

"Session of what?" they say in chorus, counting the bills.

"Accelerated literacy, by Jove!"

"Huh? You taking us for idiots or what?"

"You're gonna have to review," Diabolo insists, poker faced. "Spelling, grammar, punctuation. The whole megillah." And the three jerks go off, furious, kicking the air.

There's no way to hide it behind a haystack anymore, Diabolo's heading straight for bankruptcy. But he still has the strength of his natural optimism. That's the way he is. He dreams his life like a rock star.

"Basically, I'm just the second wife," Juliette complains, putting her head on Manu's shoulder. He was going by Moins de Mille.

"Come have a drink with me," Manu suggests.

They sit down in the Udna, facing the gallery, and order two glasses of Chardonnay. It's the most rundown café in Florentin: nothing but wobbly tables and three-legged chairs, but it has its charm, just opposite the slum. When there are great soccer matches, like the World Cup, everyone who's hip in Tel Aviv is there in front of giant screens. It's packed Friday nights, too, and the crowd overflows onto the sidewalk. It's a vestige of the old Tel Aviv, like a charm from the seventies, with the fine sense of freedom that reigned in those days before speculation took over the town.

"For Olga, great emotions and great plans, for me, a lay on the q.t.," Juliette sighs. "In secret, as a bonus. It revolts me, but . . ."

Impossible to say three sentences in a row without someone coming to interrupt her, give her a hug, talk to her about work, ask her for an appointment. She answers everyone with real kindness. Yet God knows her head is elsewhere. And then as far as contemporary art is concerned, she likes it, but basically she doesn't give a damn. She studied museology, not the market. Maybe that's why she got ahead so quickly in Tel Aviv. Her detachment, coupled with her sincere attention to the artists and their works, has attracted good painters and good people. And money's beginning to flow into her pockets, for her boss recently gave her a commission on every sale, for fear that she'd offer her services to others.

"Can I sleep at your place tonight?" Elias asks.

"Of course, but why?" Diabolo says.

"Because if I'm at your place, I won't give in to the temptation to go down to hers."

"Can I sleep at your place tonight?" Juliette asks Manu.

"Of course, but why?"

"I don't want to give in to Elias as long as he hasn't clarified the situation," she answers. "If I stay in my place, he'll show up, and I'll give in again."

# CHAPTER 26

Diabolo improvises a dinner for four on the terrace. Just with Elias, Dina, and Jonathan Simsen, his faithful assistant, but the phone doesn't stop ringing, and other friends begin to arrive in Kerem. *Friends* may be too strong a word. *Spongers* would be more accurate, and *parasites* probably too strong, but let's not quibble. In Tel Aviv, the golden rule is the more the merrier. You can't stay in a small group even at the most serious moments. Moreover, since Diabolo insists on always hosting like a lord and hiding any trace of the bad patch he's going through, Jonathan Simsen digs into the reserves of sorbets and dried fruits, scrapes the bottom of the drawers for snacks-chips-apéri-cubes, defrosts reserves of patisseries and petit fours, orders pizzas and sushi on credit, brings up the last bottles of champagne, and refills the cigar box with Cohibas as fast as it empties, like the tub of the Danaïdes. So now they are fifteen of them, somebody puts on music through the Bose, and the calm little dinner among friends turns into a party on the roof—a typical Tel Aviv party.

Romy Schneider has recovered from her back operation and drops by to say hello too. So Diabolo feels obliged to alert Manu but doesn't tell him Elias is there too. It's so obvious! When Diabo's there, so is Elias, and when Elias is there, so is Manu, you can bet on it.

Only, since Manu still has the old notion that Elias and Diabo just don't see each other anymore—or exceptionally, like the night before—he takes Juliette with him, and that's how she and Elias meet face to face despite their respective plans for avoiding each other. All that for *this*. Elias immediately stalks out of the party in a rage without even saying goodbye. Seeing them together drives him crazy. Furious. Why does Manu refuse to understand? Will he have to stop seeing him to put an end to it? His best friend, God dammit, wasting his time with Juliette without even a hope of getting laid. Is he off his rocker?

She, on the other hand, is apparently undisturbed, but this new about-turn hits her right in the face. Elias cutting out as soon as he sees her, while the night before he came inside her, in her bed, in her arms—it's too much of an outrage, and she's submerged once more by the urge to stab him. She needs to lean on Manu to calm down a little. If only he were thirty years younger! And if only she could be, not thirty years older, nor less for that matter, but if only she were a little more adventurous. She'd forget their age difference and let herself go, just on her feeling for him. But the model of her sister, Mathilde, as a materfamilias is always pressuring her, while she struggles not to faithfully reproduce the countermodel of her mother, the great puerile lover. Create a family, stop hanging around Florentin, say goodbye to her youth—that's what Juliette wants with all her strength, but at the same time she loves this life with all her heart. Beaches and white wine, bohemia and night.

Romy is also getting impatient seeing that Manu isn't leaving Juliette's side for a moment during the party, for she'd like to talk to him about something important. But Manu would rather avoid her, as he has a pretty good idea of what kind of important thing she has in mind. He doesn't know exactly how much she wants, but he knows what she wants. And he is so sick of forking out cash! Didn't he pay enough for his madness on one evening? Between the electric bike, her back operation, and a few other trifles, she's wrung him out! For the first time in his life, he's overdrawn. He also lost his left eye, which still sees only shadows. What else can she want from him?

So he accompanies Juliette everywhere, even to the bathroom. They're so intimate now. But Romy finally corners him.

"I'm renting my pad on Airbnb next week," she says. "It would be convenient to come live with you. Do you have somewhere you can go?"

"Well, no," says Manu immediately. "Where do you expect me to go?"

"Figure it out yourself!" she says, definitively odious.

"You figure it out!"

"You'll be sorry for that!"

Manu shrugs and walks away. He's had it up to here with her blackmail. Let her press charges if she wants. And let her go to hell in any case. Luckily, Juliette finds a compromise, suggesting Romy move in with her rather than Manu, and it ends that way: Romy will live at Juliette's place on Levinsky Street while Juliette goes to live with Manu on Abarbanel Street like before, but without hiding this time. Whatever Elias might say, it's just too bad.

"We can't live according to his whims," she says to Manu.

This deal suits him fine. He loves Juliette tenderly, and her presence in the house delights him, even if he's resigned to never being her lover. Unless . . . who knows if one day she won't realize that she loves him too.

# Chapter 27

That night, Elias wanders aimlessly between Cofix and Allenby, tortured by the only question that has any importance: Should he turn himself in to free Olga?

If the judge doesn't release her at the next hearing, he'll have no other option than to admit everything, make a confession, and take sole responsibility for his acts. He keeps thinking about how to get ready for that grim outcome, and it's hard. He'd never imagined that his aliyah would result in a criminal record, but anything can happen in Israel. He swindled two poor guys and sent them to jail; it can't stay like that. He's a lover, and they're criminals, OK. But still. It seems their police records are already pretty long, also OK. All the same, he's the one who swindled them, and they're the victims. They might have slit his throat, but he was lucky and got away. He must give something back for that luck, not be just lucky but lucky and just. Since Olga's attempt to put a little justice back into this business failed, that must not have been the right solution.

Another question: How can he admit his offence without involving Diabolo? Jérémie Azencot advised him to be patient and wait until Olga's next hearing before deciding what he'd tell the cops, but that wait is getting too long. Too stressful, as well.

His phone rings as he's walking into a very noisy bar on Nahalat Binyamin Street with its back to the Shuk market. A call from France. Olga's father is worried; he hasn't heard from her for three days, and "that never happens." Elias tells him Olga lost her phone when she was on assignment in the Territories, but she'll get a chip in a couple of days, and she'll call back then.

"But where is she now, right now, at this moment?"

"She's asleep," Elias answers without losing his cool. "She's working early, that's why she goes to bed early. She has to be up at five . . ."

"Wake her up, please."

"No, I can't do that, first of all I'm outside, and . . ."

"What're you doing outside at this time of night?"

"Nothing," Elias answers, taken aback, before adding, "I'm going back home . . . I promise, I'll leave a note for her to call you on my phone when she gets up."

Olga's father finally hangs up, not at all convinced, and Elias can see him landing in Tel Aviv at the end of the week to find that his daughter is in police custody. A nightmare. He'd rather be six feet under than live through something like that.

He orders a glass of Merlot and drinks it slowly, without looking at the crowd around him. However, like everywhere in Tel Aviv, there are lots of pretty girls in the bar, bunches of girls, bands of girls, mountains of girls. There's even one he doesn't notice eying him greedily, despite her Wonderbra cleavage and vermilion lipstick that makes a kind of bulb full of glowworms. Then she moves closer, but it takes her putting her hand on his thigh for him to realize she's there. She asks him to have sex with her, but her bass voice betrays her. A transvestite! Or rather transsexual, in fact, but a genuine one, with delicate wrists and a subtly thick-lipped mouth drawn with a fine pen, you might say. A miracle of plastic surgery. A prodigy of transmutation. Honestly, imitating nature to that extent takes talent!

"Three hundred to suck you off, five hundred with a shower," she suggests directly.

"You still have your dick?" Elias asks.

"Are you kidding? First of all, I never had one!" the trans claims. "Hardly a micropenis."

"What about your operation? When was it?"

"You from the Mossad or what?"

"Not at all, we're just talking."

"Me, I'm working. Ciao!"

Ordinarily, Elias would follow her or drag her off somewhere no one could see them—preferably a parking lot, a building site, or the lobby of a building, because he loves to put his head upside down with this kind of mutant. But now, he lets her go off. It seems everything has become very serious. No more joking around. And then that clandestine relationship with Juliette! Sticky like bike grease. Besides, exactly what does he want, since he hasn't wanted her for a long time? *Admit I'm crazy*, Elias says to himself. *And why don't I write all that, instead of barhopping around like an asshole? Why don't I plunge into my novel instead of taking notes that never end? As long as I was hungry, I had the strength to write, even simple notes. Now that I can eat my fill, I've dried out. Get back to feeling an empty belly.*

A text in Hebrew goes *gling!* on his cell. The cops on Dizengoff Avenue want to see him "for an affair concerning you." But what affair? He wakes up Jérémie Azencot for advice.

"Go there!" the lawyer says firmly.

"Right away?"

"As soon as possible!"

# CHAPTER 28

They walk back home arm in arm, taking Pines Street, then Shabazi, and finally up Shlush Street to Derech Yafo, the artery that separates the bourgeois-bohemian Neve Tzedek from the truly bohemian Florentin. Crossing Derech Yafo, they come upon Abarbanel Street, very badly lit at this end, with its buildings in Jerusalem stone and rusted iron hardly emerging from the shadow. It always makes Manu think of Palestine under the British mandate, before the State of Israel existed.

"It's really like a photo of 1948 Palestine here," he says to Juliette. "I love it."

"You always say that every time we get here," Juliette points out, as if they are already an old couple.

"I would have so liked to be twenty back then, join Haganah or Irgun, fire a gun . . ."

"What do you think he wants from me, exactly?" Juliette asks.

"I really don't know," Manu says distractedly. "Maybe just to screw you from time to time."

Deep in a daydream about times gone by, he doesn't realize how much this hurts her. But it does hurt Juliette. A lot. Almost as much as Elias's brusque departure from Diabolo's at the beginning of the evening. She's only his sex toy, she thinks. A hole. An object. And that revives her urge to stab him in the back. Twenty times, in fact.

"Excuse me, Jul," Manu says, almost immediately making up his carelessness by hugging her. "I was dreaming."

"No problem," says Juliette, wounded to the core.

"The surveillance tapes show you had a, let's say, personal relationship with Mrs. Elkaïm, will you confirm that?" the officer in the Dizengoff police station asks him.

"Yes—that is, personal, no, just sexual," Elias says.

"Outside of the jewelry store, did you happen to meet her?"

"Oh no, no, never," he says defensively. "It happened like that, just once and that's all."

"According to the surveillance camera, you give her cash."

"She's the one who asked me for cash," Elias claims.

"To pay for a jewel?"

"Yes, yes."

"OK," the officer says. "But on another tape, we see her giving you money. For what reason?"

"She gave me my money back for the jewel, that's all."

"So you saw each other twice?"

"Yes, twice, that's right."

"Why did she give you the money back?"

"The jewel was for a person who didn't want to be . . . well, let's say go to bed with me anymore, that's why, who didn't love me anymore."

"Who?"

"My girlfriend at the time."

"Who's that?" the cop asks.

"Her name is Olga Picard."

"You're not together anymore?"

"No, we're not," Elias says, using the piece of information Juliette gave him: Olga told the Mitzpe Ramon police that they were only coworkers.

"Can you give me her number?"

"You're not going to tell her I screwed the jeweler, at least?"

"No, no, I just want to check you're no longer together."

"What importance could that have for your investigation?"

"I'll be the judge of that," the officer answers as he gets up.

"OK," Elias says resignedly, and he gives him Olga's number.

"Wait for me right there, I'll be back."

Elias remains alone in the room, wondering how he's going to loosen this new vise, get out of this new, inexorable downward spiral. Even those two little quick lays in the jewelry store come back to smack him in the face. It proves nothing is harmless in his life anymore, everything is connected, and it's all conspiring against him.

He's being dogged by bad luck. When you screw an old woman, you don't wonder if you're being filmed! You fuck and forget. How could he imagine she'd be held up by a masked man with a French accent and the cops would look through the surveillance tapes? You'd think he's jinxed! Finding himself suspected of a second crime when he's not even out of the first one.

While he's not afraid of being accused of a holdup for any length of time—although you never know!—he's still afraid the investigation will make the connection between the jewel, Olga's detention, and the swindle he's really guilty of. The cop who's questioning him will certainly try to reach Olga. He's going to light upon his colleagues in Mitzpe Ramon, and then it's curtains for the kid. But the worst is Olga's going to learn he screwed the old jeweler lady, on top of everything else. It'll probably be all over between them. Romance, great plans, the love of his life, all thrown into the gutter. On the other hand, she's so in love, so madly in love with him. So committed, on his side, and so ready to risk anything to get him off. Maybe she'll understand that's the way the man she loves is made, but he's the one she loves. The bad luck that's hounding him can also give a woman the desire to be his companion through hard times, fight for him to her last breath. There must be Greek tragedies built on this kind of fatal destiny. *Greek bastards who destroyed the first temple in Jerusalem,* thinks Elias immediately. Well, not exactly destroyed but worse still: disfigured, perverted, demonized by building a gymnasium just beneath it, so their cult of the body and their fucking ephebes could triumph over the people of the book.

The officer comes back into the room a few minutes later and sits down behind the desk again to announce that he was unable to reach Olga as her phone went to voice mail. Elias breathes an imperceptible sigh of relief. The Mitzpe Ramon cops must have turned off his darling's smartphone, so the cops in Tel Aviv can't learn Olga is in the hands of their colleagues to the south. Yet.

"Just a detail," the cop says. "How much did you pay for the jewel she reimbursed you for?"

"I don't remember," Elias claims.

"Please try."

"Seven thousand shekels, I think."

"You're sure?"

"Well, no. I don't remember very well."

"Because the jeweler said you paid a lot more, but she only reimbursed you for part of it."

"Yes, she's a thief!"

"So by any chance, would you have wanted to recover the difference between what you paid for it and what she reimbursed?"

"Oh yes! But I didn't have the bill, since it was in cash. I had no proof."

"I mean, recover that money by force."

"That's absurd! I'm a journalist, not a holdup man!" Elias shouts.

"In fact, you paid eighteen thousand shekels for that jewel."

"That's possible," Elias says distractedly.

"And in fact, that's the sum of cash that was stolen from her."

"So what does that prove? Confront us, and we'll see!"

Another police officer enters the room, holding a piece of paper in his hand, which he gives to his colleague.

"Right, the judge issued a search warrant. Would you rather give me the keys to your apartment or go along with us?"

"I want my lawyer!"

"OK, I'll notify him," the cop answers as he gets up. "You have his contact info?"

He walks out of the room, leaving Elias alone on the chair again but free to move around. Aside from the table the cop cleared off, there's absolutely nothing else in the room, not even a magazine to read. That's a principle when someone is held for questioning all over the earth: between two interrogations, leave the suspect to himself to provoke introspection and get a confession out of him.

But Elias analyzes the situation differently. In fact, it's more a revelation than an analysis. A terribly upsetting revelation, because he can easily see there's poetic justice in it: he's accused of a crime he didn't commit, whereas he's guilty of another crime that he's not being blamed for at all. Is this just? Unjust? Or simply absurd? The truth is he didn't hold up the jeweler, while he did swindle the Bedouins, but since the jeweler had swindled him and the Bedouins wanted to cut his throat, he tells himself that justice, real justice, consists in judging the whole business and the guilt of each party. For in this affair everyone is both guilty and victim, sort of like the wonderful song by Gérald de Palmas.

What would be just would be for Olga to be released and the jeweler arrested for fiscal fraud and making a false accusation. What would be even more just would be for the Bedouins to be released but remain accused of attempted murder. What would be still more just would be that since everyone is both guilty and a victim, they all be set free and the whole thing forgotten. Wipe the slate clean. Except for the jeweler, maybe. What a bitch! *And then no, why not set her free, too,* Elias tells himself. After all, he did like screwing her the first time. The second was unpleasant, but not to the point where he'd want to harm her.

Only, his indulgent daydream will remain a hollow dream, for the law knows only innocent people and guilty people, not both at the same time. But his strongest feeling is that immanent justice has finally found the right form for it. And it could thus cut the Gordian knot that was strangling him. All that took some time, but there you are. From now on, the two pans of the scale will be at the same level. Something fair is finally taking shape. He'll no longer have a crisis of conscience. Elias is ready to pay for something he did not commit, since he was not able to pay for what he did.

# CHAPTER 29

Jérémie Azencot has obtained Olga's release without a charge, since the police could not produce material evidence of a connection to Elias beyond professional. A real stroke of luck! For there actually was a piece of evidence—within their grasp, in fact: her WhatsApp voice mail. They would have found Elias's announcement that they became a couple on November 13. The WhatsApp group they created when they got back together would have given them away. Not to mention the love notes they exchanged every day. But the cops would have had to get a translation, and they didn't. Therefore, the judge ordered the accused to be released.

Always a bit of a braggart and protective, Jérémie holds her by the arm as they leave the courthouse in Mitzpe Ramon, but he doesn't yet know how to tell her the bad news. Having to tell her Elias is accused of a holdup does spoil the moment he was so impatiently waiting for since the first hearing. It might be easier to tell her when they're squeezed into the Cinquecento. And then the presence of Diabolo will give him a little courage, he hopes. Or else Diabolo will make the sacrifice.

But since Olga must first get back the twenty-seven thousand shekels and her phone and the rented Audi, he walks her to the police station, while Diabolo goes back to Tel Aviv alone, drawing on one of the last Montecristos from the cigar box. Good old Diabolo! As megalomaniacal as he is helpful, as much a godfather by nature as a good little soldier when circumstances require. The lawyer suggests that he drive the convertible, but Olga would rather take the wheel herself, claiming she isn't insured for a second driver. Actually, it's because after four nights in jail, she really feels like driving in the open air with her hair in the wind, through the blond ochre landscapes of the Negev.

Before she starts up, she tries to get Elias, but she gets his voice mail, and that upsets her a little. She misses him so much! She glances at the eighty text messages she got while she was held for questioning but doesn't read them right away. In the bunch, there are at least twenty from her father. Increasingly alarmed messages as the days go by. So she calls him first to reassure him.

"You got a chip, darling?" her dad asks.

"No, why?"

"Elias told me you had to get one."

"Oh yes, yes, of course, but . . . I don't have the time to talk to you about it now. I'm on assignment," she claims. "I'll call this afternoon."

"You're calling from a new phone, that it?"

"Why new?" Olga asks at first, surprised, and immediately catches herself. "Oh yes, you bet, I have a brand-new, um, Samsung, really new, ultranew even, you know, the . . ."

"Galaxy 7?"

"Yeah, that's it, a Galaxy 7 . . . I had to change the . . . well, anyway, actually, I'll explain everything to you later . . . love you, Dad."

She starts the car, somewhat stressed but showing nothing, while Azencot is still trying to find the words to tell her that her man is in the prison of Ramla.

They drive along in silence for twenty miles or so after exchanging a few banalities about Audis, the desert, the best bars in Tel Aviv, and then stop for gas in the middle of nowhere, at the turnoff for Midreshet Ben-Gurion, leading to the Sde Boker kibbutz where the founder of the State of Israel is buried. A gas station on the moon would have approximately the same effect. Jérémie tells himself it's the right moment and a fitting place to spill the beans, but first they go buy a bottle of mineral water in the store. As they walk out, just before getting into the car, Azencot takes Olga's hand, looks her straight in the eye, and finally says: "Olga, I have bad news . . . be strong . . . you're not going to see Elias right away. There . . . it is my duty to inform you: he is in prison."

Not a word more at the moment, so Olga can take in the first blow, and in fact tears begin to flow down the young woman's face. She doesn't answer at all, doesn't even ask a question, convinced as she is that it's all her fault, the fault of her wretched expedition. She doesn't know what happened to Elias yet. She still doesn't know he's been wrongly accused of holding up the jeweler on Dizengoff. She just imagines he turned himself in to free her, and she feels guilty—unforgivable, even.

So she gives the keys of the car to Jérémie and sinks into the passenger seat with her head in her hands. The lawyer sits down behind the wheel, clearing his throat, but doesn't start right away, leaning over her. Seeing her in tears moves him like all hell. Why is this client's emotion so communicative, for godsake? Usually he doesn't give a flying fuck. He never has the slightest desire to cry over the fate of his clients, and when it does happen, he swallows his tears easily. Now, and not only now, but since the first hearing, since the first time he saw her, Olga has made a great impression on him. Whether she's unmoved or in tears, something powerful emanates from her and touches him.

He takes her hand again without taking his eyes off her for a second. "I'm going to get him out of there, don't worry," he promises, reluctantly, for actually if Elias were out of the picture, it would suit him just fine. Mind you, he likes Elias—but he's so attracted to Olga! Yet Jérémie's twenty years older than she is. All the same, she makes his heart beat like a teenager's.

"Start the car, please," she asks him with a sob.

Her unhappiness crushes all her thoughts for miles, like a concrete screed laid over flowering water lilies. Nothing emerges, and nothing comes to mind except that she won't be seeing Elias. Not right away in any case, and she seems to see an endless road opening up before her. But little by little, she orders things in her mind. She thought herself too strong, too crafty, by imagining that all she had to do was entrap Kirzenbaum to turn the situation around. Yet her stratagem worked. It was well thought out, well conceived, and well executed. What went wrong was luck, the little grain of sand that jammed the whole machine. If they'd gotten to the trail three minutes later, just three minutes later, they wouldn't have crossed paths with the cops, and that would have changed everything. Not even three minutes, in fact—just a minute later. But chance counts too. It saves or dooms an enterprise, transforms a dream into a nightmare, a defeat into victory, a good deed into a crime. Fucking chance! One time it's on your side, another time it's against you. So unpredictable and so unreliable! "Leave nothing to chance"—that doesn't mean a thing. Chance remains the unpredictable master of all our acts. The deus ex machina. That's what she realizes on this day. It doesn't prevent her from being unhappy, but it helps her to see more clearly.

After Be'er Sheva, the gateway to the Negev, she recovers her confidence and asks Jérémie to let her drive again. The lawyer immediately takes the passenger seat. He senses that she's already out of her affliction and she's now thinking of her next move. She's quick and synthesizes well, this girl—impervious to emotionalism. But she doesn't know everything. She doesn't have all the cards in her hand, and it would be too cruel, too risky, to tell her only now why Elias has been incarcerated. She might crack all at once this time, go into a tailspin. Can't think she's made of reinforced concrete. So he lets her drive to the outskirts of Tel Aviv without saying much, just with Israeli rap on the speakers, promising himself to tell her when they get there. But once they're in front of his office on Frishman Street, he still can't find his words, while Olga takes the twenty-seven thousand shekels out of her purse and gives them to him. "Here, that's all I have," she says, but the lawyer pushes away the money.

"We'll see about that afterward," he says grandly, and he leaves her without having been able to tell her the reason Elias is now behind bars but vowing to tell her on the phone a little later. He's still staring at her rather pointedly, while she's impatient to leave.

Decidedly, this girl is making him lose the exact science of seduction. Never has he felt like such a klutz.

Olga returns the Audi to the car2go agency on HaYarkon Street and then walks back down toward the Tayelet and grabs a cab to go to Florentin along the coast. She gets off on Abarbanel Street in front of the Moins de Mille gallery even before going to take a shower. She wants to see Juliette. The trauma of their arrest created an exceptional feeling between them. Something strong—unbreakable, no doubt. Juliette already experienced that in the army with her girlfriends in the regiment. For Olga, this is the first time she's felt such a surge of emotion for another girl.

As soon as she sees her, Juliette drops the sale she's concluding and throws herself into her arms. Their hug is so long, so tender, that everybody in the shop is stunned: owner and clients alike, the artists who're there, and even the passersby outside. They all look at them wide eyed. All of them are choked up, without understanding why. In Tel Aviv, a hug is more frequent and banal than a handshake or a kiss on the cheek, but this one is so intense they can't stop watching it, even if there's a bit of voyeurism in that. It's just beautiful to see, that's all, and you can't turn your eyes away from what is beautiful—such tenderness, the impression of a truly unique love. People like to see great emotions expressed freely and, what's more, by two such beautiful girls. And it lasts, it lasts, it lasts like something that's too much, a wait that was too long, something that was inexhaustible and refused to be slaked. Hardly do they let each other go, to laugh and cry for a moment, than they hug each other again and kiss each other like good bread, saying, "Oh, wow," while around them the people remain smiling, indulgent, won over.

They have to go outside and walk away from the gallery to be alone, with no witness, with a bit of vocabulary now and not just the little sounds and reflexive cries that leak out of their throats.

"It's just unbelievable . . . they released you!" Juliette says, beaming. "I'm so, so glad! Come on, we'll go to the French Bakery."

"No, no, let's go to the Landwer Café," Olga suggests, taking her hand. "I love their Limonana."

"I really thought you wouldn't come back, I swear! I was sick over it."

"I don't even have your number!"

"And I don't have yours!" Juliette answers in a burst of laughter.

They sit down hand in hand, like two little Tel Aviv lesbians, on the glider of the Landwer Café, at the foot of the Beans and Abarbanel Street. It's the seat reserved for lovers, that glider. And they order a *café Affour* for Juliette and a Limonana for Olga.

"I don't smell too bad?"

"It's sort of OK," Juliette confesses, giggling.

"Isn't that just meshugga, they prevent you from washing when you're held for questioning?" Olga says, hugging her and squeezing her hard against her body.

"OK, but tell me, how'd you get out?" Juliette whispers into her ear.

She doesn't have time to answer the question, Jérémie's calling her back.

"Chhhkh," she sighs. "Can't get rid of this guy."

"Who is it?"

"The lawyer, Jérémie."

"It may be important," Juliette says.

"I'll call you back," Olga says, cutting him off. "Well, I lucked out," she continues, putting her smartphone away. "Madame Benshimoun was marrying off her daughter, so she didn't have time to do the job."

"Huh? What *is* this business?" Juliette guffaws. "Who's Madame Benshimoun?"

"The translator. They asked her to translate my WhatsApp, but she didn't turn in her work in time."

"Oh, brilliant! She saved your life. You should send her a little present."

"But I don't know her. It's the cops who told me."

They hug again, hold hands, smile at each other, kiss without embarrassment or afterthoughts, but both of them can feel they're only avoiding and postponing the subject that's brought them so close but could make them angry too. Loving the same man is a very bad idea, whatever Jules and Jim might say. Elias is an explosive subject. They hardly touched on it before they were separated by the Mitzpe Ramon cops, but they'll certainly have to talk about it and really talk about it this time. All the time she was in detention, Olga never stopped thinking about it: Why did Elias never tell her about Juliette?

At this moment, neither of them knows why he's in prison, and Juliette doesn't even know he's there. So she doesn't understand why Olga ran to see her first. Normally when you love a man the way she loves Elias, he's the one you run to first. But Juliette doesn't dare ask the question, of course.

"OK, to the shower!" she says like a Scout troop leader as she gets up.

"No, wait a little! This sun is too nice," Olga answers. "In a month it'll be frying us like potatoes, let's take advantage of it!"

They leave the Landwer to walk to Olga's in Yafo and get there in less than ten minutes. *Where can Elias be?* Juliette still wonders. Would he be waiting for them there? And she prepares herself for this improbable encounter. He'll be flabbergasted when he sees her, of course. So all through the walk, she tries to master her anger at him. On the other hand, it's a pleasure not to have to hide anymore, not to have to see him on the q.t. when Olga disappears for a day or so. On the way, Jérémie calls again, but Olga still doesn't pick up.

"He's really bugging me now!"

"It's the lawyer again?" Juliette worries.

"Yeah, and he doesn't even want me to pay him, don't you think that's fishy?"

"He's in love."

"You got it, girl!"

But Elias is not at Olga's, and this absence is starting to make Juliette anxious. What if he comes back all of a sudden and finds her there? She makes a few phone calls to make herself look busy. She calls artists who asked her for an appointment—that disguises her edginess—and then the gallery, to notify them she'll be back in only in the early afternoon, and her boss is concerned she dropped a client in the middle of a sale just to follow her girlfriend. "Don't worry, he'll be back," she answers, without justifying herself any more than that. She hangs up savoring the new status she's gained at work. She does what she wants, she comes and goes, she gets there at no particular time and leaves when she feels like it. A real diva. As long as she stays, her boss must tell himself, to accept behavior like that. But at every step on the landing of the stairs, she shudders.

Olga comes out of the shower fifteen minutes later, after using all the hot water in the tank.

"They didn't want to tell me if they'd released you or not, can you imagine?" she says, knotting a towel around her hair. "I could see you weren't in the other cells as I went by, and that was a relief, but at the same time I was so mad at myself for getting you into this shit, oh my God!"

Olga goes into her room, pulls clean clothes out of the closet, and spreads them out on her bed, smiling.

What a joy to be able to pick what you're going to put on, just think of it! Yes, that makes her smile: this kind of thing is so trivial in ordinary life but so extraordinary after captivity. She drops her bath towel without hiding from Juliette and puts on panties, a black miniskirt, and a T-shirt, while Juliette senses the moment is approaching when she'll have to tell her about the evening that followed her return to Tel Aviv. How can she avoid it? But she's such a bad liar!

"I hope we'll be able to make that trip together again," she says to change the subject.

"Oh yes," Olga answers, "the desert is so beautiful."

"You know, still further south, there are landscapes that look like the surface of the moon."

"You're not hungry?" Olga asks.

They go down to eat a salad in the pedestrian shopping street below the building, and of course Olga finally asks her what she did when she got back to Tel Aviv the previous Saturday night.

"You must've called Manu when you got back, right?"

"Not right away, no," Juliette answers, somewhat taken aback. "I was exhausted, I just wanted to sleep."

"Poor Jul! It must have been awful to go back in that bus," Olga says sympathetically.

"Especially after what happened to us."

"And the next day, you did call him, finally?"

"Umm, well, no," Juliette admits, embarrassed. "No, no, the next day not at all, I waited for him to . . . well, I mean, here's what happened: I bumped into him as I was going to work, that's what . . . and he already knew, can you believe it?"

Olga takes her hand again and squeezes it hard in hers, without trying to find out if she called Elias or not that night. Or the next day. At one time or another, in any case. Decidedly, the topic is too hot to touch. She can see it by Juliette's embarrassment as soon as they get near the theme, so she creates a diversion by bringing up her return to work.

"I'll go there tomorrow," Olga says. "You can't just go straight from jail to job. You think I'll be able to get back into it easily, Jul? I'm so afraid they'll look at me like I have the plague."

"Don't worry about it, that's not the most important thing for the moment."

"No, that's true," Olga admits. Suddenly she takes the bull by the horns. "You know about Elias?"

"Know what?"

"He's in prison, Manu didn't tell you?"

"No!" Juliette exclaims, with tears in her eyes. "He finally gave himself up?"

Her heartbeats turn into palpitations. She can't stop herself from thinking again of that night, always the same night, when she advised him to turn himself in, a night she'd like to erase from her memory forever, a night of betrayal and a second wife . . . but a delightful night, too—her last night of love and pleasure with the man she loves. Yet she'd rather never have lived through it. Now she thinks Elias followed her advice, and she has a funny feeling. Something like gratitude. Well, no, not gratitude, but something like that: respect. *There*, she tells herself, *for once he listened to me, for once he respected me.* So all her reproaches fade into the background, far, far behind this feeling. All her reproaches are now obsolete. Not that she no longer resents Elias, but an injustice has been repaired. Her urge to stab him erased like chalk on a blackboard. She feels pacified, even if that last night of love with him still lurks in a corner of her mind like a delight and a reproach, both. One day, perhaps, she'll have the strength to confess it to Olga. Then everything will be tender again, then everything will be fine.

# THE END

# ABOUT THE AUTHOR

*Photo © 2019 Fabrice Calvo*

Marco Koskas, the author of fifteen books, was born in Tunisia, grew up in France, and now lives in Israel. In 1979, his novel *Balace Bounel* won the Prix du Premier Roman, and he was a fellow of the French Academy in Rome from 1980 to 1982. In 2012, reviewing *Mon cœur de père* (Éditions Fayard), Patrick Besson wrote in *Le Point*: "Koskas is a fighter for his own style. He has remained raw as a Tartar warrior." In 2018, after being rejected by numerous publishers, Koskas self-published *Goodbye Paris, Shalom Tel Aviv* on CreateSpace, and the novel was short-listed for France's prestigious Prix Renaudot.

# ABOUT THE TRANSLATOR

*Photo © 2009 Nicole Ball*

David Ball is professor emeritus of French and comparative literature, Smith College. He was named Chevalier dans l'Ordre des Palmes Academiques by the French Republic in 2017. He was president of the American Literary Translators Association from 2003 to 2005. His *Darkness Moves: An Henri Michaux Anthology 1927–1982* won the MLA's award for outstanding literary translation in 1995, and his Jean Guéhenno *Diary of the Dark Years: 1940–1944* won the French-American Foundation 2014 prize for translation (nonfiction).